FREE WILL
from Lockdown

A Multiverse Love Story

SHASHIKIRAN ALUR

ISBN
Paperback: 979-8-88733-034-1
Hardcase: 979-8-88772-977-0

CONTENTS

FOREWORD

I owe this book, the first amongst my many to come, to my mother K Vasanthi J Ram — an amazing storyteller, who never wrote them down or published them. But she's inspired some who love her to become authors.

My book — its conception, concoction, completion, and publication couldn't have been possible without the constant boosts of confidence, some beta reading, and expert insights of Dr Sunita Jakhar.

A special thanks to M Sudha for providing a reality check about the story I wanted to tell.

And to my dad, the esteemed litterateur, who inspired me by not being impressed.

PREFACE

Years ago, a colleague of mine who doesn't turn a blind eye to the paranormal, went for a honeymoon to Sicily. Her husband, without whom the honeymoon would've been just a vacation, does turn a blind eye and often dismisses any allusions to anything unexplainable. On their first day in Catania, they went to watch a movie in a cinema hall. I will stay away from questioning the futility of visiting a cinema hall in Sicily – a mesmerizing island where so many other sites and pass-times offer more tantalizing options.

To keep it short, the husband went to the men's room during the movie and on his return to his seat, he was a changed man.

"Katrin, I have been to this cinema hall before. I knew exactly where the toilets were, I didn't look for the signs. I knew the layout of the room, the color of the walls, and everything there!"

My colleague whispered back, "But you have never been to Sicily before!"

His eyes glowed in the darkness as he replied, equally miffed, "Exactly my point!"

Maybe he did visit Sicily after all?! A different life, a different he.

If two lockdowns in this pandemic have taught me something, it is how I could have used the first lockdown differently and how that might have made life in the second lockdown better.

Or maybe I did. I just don't know that. Not the I that writes this book.

I

SHE SAID – NEERAJA
(Neeraja Kashyap Babbitt)

So that's it then. The votes are in. I am going to go ahead with it.

I got 107 comments back. And every one of them is on my side. I eagerly search for a Cassandra. Not a single one out there. I even scan for words like, "Are you sure?" or "Do you want to think about it?" — a word or two of caution.

None. And that in itself is something. No?

The 223 emojis are all in my favor. An overwhelming 135 of 😨, 70 of 👍 and 👍 from the more racially woke. I even got a dozen variants of the hearts, but that's just from my peeps. My coffee peeps from the yoga studio. We always find time to hang out after yoga. Or rather, used to hang out. Before the confounded lockdown.

But it's not the whimsical emojis that swung my decision. Who do you think I am? A floozie? I am actually basing it on the 34 valuable comments. All in my support. They were brief but supportive. Did they lack a level of empathy one expects from the gravity of my query? Perhaps. But then, who these days wants to show too much of it on a social network anyway? What with all the greedy corporations mining data like prospectors during the Gold Rush!

The comments did give me enough to go with.

Some said, "We feel ya!"

And then there were those who said, "Wishing you the best" or "You will come through" or a simple Mmuuahhh! Proud of ya".

All in all, it was unanimous support for my post on Facebook — 'Seeking recommendations for a good divorce lawyer'.

Something that has been on my mind for the last few weeks.

And then I read this piece in HuffPost — 'What's better for the kids? Incompatible parents staying together or divorced but happily single parents?'. That's when I decided to get recommendations on Facebook.

And I also got some good attorney recommendations on my post.

Not on my status update! Good Gosh no! How can you think that?! I am not the one who puts my life on public display. What am I? An exhibitionist?

Will seems to think I am. A closet exhibitionist at least, and maybe I am. Just enough to give me the kicks when we make furtive love on park benches after dark. Just the notion of it, that someone at the wrong place at the wrong time may be watching is quite a thrill in itself. But putting my intimacy on full display? Never! Everything we ever did was in the blanket of darkness or abandoned places. The exhibition was purely notional. That 'What If?' thing. Will brought it to me. So, if he says, I am a closet exhibitionist, he is an accessory to it. And honestly, he could talk me into it now. If only Will still had it in him. He used to be so excited about it when I would suggest something like that — shyly back in the days we were dating, right after Grad school. And later, unabashedly so. Perhaps, I wanted to tear to shreds my repressed sexuality, so tightly enchained through my adolescence.

I could make love to him on our front lawn tonight —at the drop of a pen! No doubt about that.

The caveats remain: 1) Almost everyone from the neighborhood is out for Memorial Day weekend. 2) We disable the motion sensor for the garden lights. 3) The kids are at my friend Aditi and Sharan's home.

Whatever happened to that part of us? When did all that stop? It is this cursed pandemic and the ensuing lockdowns. The divide it has brought between us. That I am sure.

And now, Memorial Day has come and gone. None of our neighbors from the entire cul-de-sac even left town. Everyone is hunkered down. It is risky getting out and catching an infection. Better to stay home. And so, the chance for our notional shamelessness fizzled out of sheer lack of initiative. Will's lethargy.

Perhaps it is what triggered me to post my query quite discreetly in a closed Facebook group.

I had given it quite a bit of thought for a couple of weeks. Deep thought. Thoughts that have cost me many nights of sleep. Sleep chased away by Will's snores.

I don't get much rest in the daytime anyway. With this whole work-from-home concept. I am just happy to keep my job, while millions have lost theirs and some, their businesses as well. But I don't venture out much anymore. I feel less adventurous venturing into the cesspool of the air contaminated with variant after variant of the bug.

The lockdowns and the restrictions have put everything in a topsy-turvy situation. There is too much to do. Even when everyone is mostly home. Especially because everyone is home. All the time. And it is crazy. 24/7. It still is.

It is overwhelming. I had not signed up for this. I don't mean Mika and Mohini. Not my adorable dolls. I could sign up for spending a hundred years with them, anytime, in any given birth over and over again. I could sign up all over again for them. The annoying morning sickness, months of mood swings, and bloating. Everything of that was a divine gift. Mika and Mohini are my primordial raison d'être.

I mean Will. The Will from the lockdown, I should say.

Until the lockdowns, I always thought I had signed up for everything life would offer us. I actually always believed in that one love. Will *was* that one love.

OMG! I just referred to Willie as Will and IS as WAS! My mind IS already made up on the divorce! And here I was thinking that I was posting just to explore.

Stella had warned me rather grudgingly, "Marriages mostly end up bad even if the relationships feel great. It's the man. A few years and a kid or two later, you start living the man with all the kinks you thought you could straighten out. It becomes all about the kids and in the end just them."

She has always been cynical. But then, she is a victim of abuse. Abused by men in life — an ex-husband, a stepfather, and others. And then, sexually assaulted by her ex-boss, long ago.

Will thinks she's lying about the assault.

"She just wants her two minutes of fame," he dismisses it, just because that ex-boss is his preferred candidate now running for office – the most important one.

"Have you seen how she dresses? And her pictures on TV? Whoa! What was she thinking dressed like that at work?! Even if the assault happened, which I bet it didn't, I am sure she was trying to seduce the Senator and something went awry."

Spoken like a man. It's never a man's fault. It's always the woman to blame.

They have this weird animosity for each other — my Will and Stella, even though they don't know each other. He cannot stand the name of her — as if she is some portent.

I believe Stella. She may be cynical, but she is genuine. I used to intern for her during my graduate studies. She was such a great mentor. And even back then I knew something had gone wrong in her earlier job. And finally, she went to the press last month after almost two decades. She had messaged me ahead of time, a subtle hint. "I may stir a few headlines soon. Just want to give you a heads up." She's always been in touch. We chat about everything. She still counsels me about everything.

"You need to find yourself an escape room during these times, Neeraja," she'd advised me almost a year ago, before the second lockdown. "Marriages will face the toughest tests during the lockdown." And what a prophesy it has been!

OMG! The Universe is guiding me towards divorce.

It is not that I have fallen out of love with Will. I don't see the difference between falling in love and loving someone. And if there is no falling in love, there cannot be a falling out of it.

We were meant to be, I thought, we were meant to be together. Together forever. But after the two lockdowns, and the narrow window of relief in between when the hypocrisy of it all lay bare, it is clear to me now.

The world in crisis has not been helpful to anyone. Especially not to us. The kids are disoriented with all that is going on. They perceive it. And then there is Willie.

The lockdown exposed him, I should say.

"Willie…" I call out to him from my desk in our bedroom, my workspace now.

Silence.

"Willie…"

Silence again.

"Willie… I know you are by the patio."

Still no answer.

How could he NOT be home? We are in a lockdown! We can hardly step outside, even if Will does not want to abide. He always finds excuses to step out. There is that pent-up urge not to comply. If one should NOT step out, he HAS to. He is just not a responsible citizen of society. Too much about personal freedom. He has to try and defy rules laid out for the greater good of society. Why can't he just stay put? Comply and pay heed to lessen the risk on us, and to others. To the world at large.

But I did not complain. I was glad when he would step out. He would take Mohini and Mika with him. My poor angels! They were traumatized by these bizarre phases where everyone stayed home. They still are. At least we adults can rationalize. We can talk ourselves out of it. But we haven't done a great job of that either. There has been no precedent to prepare us for this situation. But the kids? It drove them crazy — the sudden confinement, all friends hiding. Mika tried to tide over it. As the older one, she knew she needed to set an example. It was evident in her eyes though. And that got li'l Mohini going. Even the games in our green backyard didn't help. Why couldn't Chiki and Angie come over? Why couldn't she go? Why wasn't anyone ever coming? It was very puzzling for her.

Will did take them out with him. He is a responsible dad that way — a loving father. But then he did get his way both times – daughters! Two for two! I wouldn't have minded a son. It didn't matter to me. But he was fervently praying for a daughter both times.

"Why would I want a son? I know what an asshole I was growing up. Why would I want to see that again?!" That's his argument.

"Maybe as a better parent and your son won't be an asshole," I had counterargued.

"So you agree that I am an asshole?"

"Of course honey! I always agree with you."

Those were still the days when I loved everything about him wholeheartedly. It was that phase. I still love him in wholeness, but sometimes not wholeheartedly. There is a difference. That was unconditional love, now I have my conditions. And wait till this divorce gets finalized, that's when he will face even more conditions.

Although, I don't think I will be a bitch about it. There's not going to be "see you in hell!" or "see you in court". That's too dramatic. It's for the stupid movies. I have no wish not to see him till eternity or the Day of Judgement. We have a word for it in my mother tongue – *Qayamat*, although in my supposed religion these judgments are not to be made. Just a gentle suggestion. No commandments nor edicts with a Thump of Totem and a "Thou shalt not..."

I don't judge him even now when his lack of communal responsibility is exposed. I just don't want my daughters exposed to that side of him.

He is still going to be Mika and Mohini's father. I have no intention of keeping him away from them. I just want to keep them away from his 'each to his own' philosophy. If this 24/7 duress has taught me anything, it is this.

Good Gosh! I need to figure out the mechanics of it. About how we continue after the divorce.

"Willie!" I raise my voice a few notches, but this was before I ever thought about the D-word.

Still no reply.

I switch my webcam off and mute myself from my Zoom meeting.

"I am done!" Mohini's triumphant voice from the toilet persists.

I jab in a quick 'brb' on the keyboard to my boss. She understands the hazards of working from home. She has two teenage kids. I get a thumbs up and a wink emoji back from her.

I rush to attend to Mohini, as she continues to play with her rag doll, quite comfortable on her potty seat. It's her first few days of potty training.

And Willie continues to languish on the recliner, right by the patio door, just 10 feet away from the toilet! Shamelessly immersed in clipping his nails — making an assortment of it on a plate. Like some mezze platter at a neo-fusion Mediterranean restaurant. Not just that! He does that with his eyebrow hair that he plucks out regularly. A fascination to collect his discarded body scales. Some serpentine obsession. Disgusting!

And then there are his perennial pant-less serenades. He even attends his work videoconferences like that.

"The camera doesn't go that low Neera!" As if that is an excuse to cavort around in his boxers. In some ways, he has not come out of his undergrad days. Thank God, I didn't know him back then. In Grad school, his sense of humor had floored me.

"Charlie Rose was so good. Wasn't he brilliant in his feature on 'The Namesake'?! Always spiffy in his choice of clothes. So engaging with his guests," I had remarked at our study club back then.

"I bet he was just doing a number on Jhumpa" was Willie's smart-aleck comment.

"Why else would she be so engaging to them? C'mon! There's something weird about him and his frames. Some kind of see-through lenses," he had remarked snidely. We all burst into peals of laughter.

As a joke, it was funny — Farrelly Brothers kind of humor. But because it was so long before Charlie Rose was outed.

No longer a joke. Was he like this before? Did I just not notice it? So in love that I was.

Withholding information willfully is a deliberate act of deception. It is not just about clothes not worn in a Zoom call. In our visits to National parks, he would misstate Mika's and now Mohini's age.

"They can't tell the difference," he would claim.

It is the example he sets for the girls.

And then there is that look of disbelief in his eyes as I am tidying up the whole house before we leave town for the National Parks. Doesn't even lend a hand!

"What?" He laughs incredulously. "Why do you care so much about leaving a good impression for the burglars who break in?"

He has no qualms about leaving a mess behind when we are out of town.

Sloppy not just in his attitude but his appearance as well. Especially these days.

Why can't he care more about his appearance, even if he is at home? At least for me? For his 'wifey' – as he calls me. Yep, that's what he calls me when my parents are visiting. He has this illusion that my parents speak only colonial English. Admittedly, Daddy does crack up when Willie calls me wifey. But Daddy comes from the era that sees the woman as a 'wifey' anyway. They do get along well though – Daddy and Willie. He's such a sweet host when my parents visit. Over three-four months at a time and not a groan or a grumble! He loves their company, even if his hours at work get a little longer and his pub nights more frequent.

He may not be as hands-on about Indian culture and rituals as Amma expects him to be. But he is a good son-in-law. At least Daddy thinks so. Amma may not like him lending a hand at home, but my Willie is a man of today. He shares everything with me including our chores, more than Daddy ever did. It didn't even matter to Daddy that Amma was teaching full-time at a college. But those were different times, a different place, and a different generation.

Amma regrets that I did not marry an Indian – an arranged marriage. Ten years, and she still thinks about it. She'll let the occasional remark slip out in Hindi. Willie can't understand. Nothing nasty though. I wouldn't have it that way.

For being so welcoming to his in-laws for four months at a time, I have to say he is a star!

"It may be expected out of an Indian husband, but for Will, it is exemplary" is what Sarita says. My kid sister adores Willie. She had a huge crush on him when he visited India. I remember her eyes lighting up like some football practice ground floodlights. She was just thirteen, but that was twelve years ago. Now she insists only on Indians. She is engaged to one. Like most who come to the US to study but stick to Indian. Not just in the food but also in the men. At least with food, it is the spices. It numbs our palate. But with men? Why? Such frogs in the well. Expecting a certain kind of compliance from their wife towards the family. It is not that they are any more macho. Men will be men, everywhere – any color. Born with a 'male privilege', while complaining about how we women have it easy.

The flavors may be cultural but the dominant aftertaste of privilege is ubiquitous. Indian men of this generation have definitely piped it down – especially the higher educated ones in the Indian mega-cities who insist on English as their main language. Except when in extended family get-togethers in India. The Indian way in India. Male ego, in all its variations in all the cultures.

It's not just us humans – it's every species. Well, at least the species that have some brains. And now the enlightened proponents of equality 'bling off' their male privilege. Just the humans. You know the kind, who are forced to acknowledge equality but cannot forego the privileges they have inherited.

No different for Indian men. The adage, 'You can take an Indian out of India but not India out of an Indian' is a valuable truth. I guess one can 'find & replace' it with any ethnicity. Armenian – Kasparian, an Italian Tucci.

It's not just men. We are all frogs in our cozy wells. Pining to jump into our native ponds – much warmer ponds than the nearby frozen finger lakes. Like Labradors throwing themselves to swim in every given excuse of a pond. I live it in many ways – the

Indian-ness. After ten years married to a white man, I can't give it up, where I don't want to. But my Indian friends with Indian spouses have more of that Indian. It is like a cult. A geographically distributed worldwide cult. *www.Indian.co.in* — a cult stronger than Pappa Y's Nazarene commune in California. Willie's ex-mentor from a decade ago.

Perhaps it is just a diaspora thing. 'Birds of a feather flock together'. I have a tendency to exaggerate. We all do. Especially us liberals in America. For us liberals, every observation by a white person, even in jest, is racist. Could be about any race! Even their own. The more incisive it is, the worse is the label. A Nazi. Or a Klan member. Poor Will can never build on the cultural jokes I concoct at parties. While I languish in my unWhite privilege — a longer leash on racial judgments. I see the eagerness in his eyes, his lips quivering to finish my racial quips. A fire raging on his tongue-tip to leap out. One tongue to the other. Tongue in cheek. Poor Will is duct-taped for being a white man. Condemned from making such jokes. Somehow we liberals find our thrills in exaggerating our typecasts. The Indian families would be shell-shocked!

But I cannot have any of that – Indian families huddling into diasporic ghettoes. We could have our very armbands of Swastika – reversed. When my parents are visiting, I have to rip off that band though. There is that compliance thing. Being born to a culture of 1.3 billion and 3500 years old adds a lot of weight to the cross we bear. And the cross becomes heavier for the women, even girls. And no male world comes forth with chivalry to carry our cross load. I still carry that cross, especially when I am visiting India or when India is visiting me.

I remember how shocked Willie was when he saw me in my schizophrenic Indian identity, the first time we visited India together. The time Sarita went googly-eyed.

It was not a meet-the-parents thing. Not then. We had been dating less than a year. I wasn't even sure if he was the one. I probably did but it was still too early. For my parents, he was 'a friend' visiting. He was to fly to Pune at the urging of Pappa Y. Pappa Y had asked him to check prospects for extending his Nazarene commune into India. Imagine! A neo-evangelical new-age Nazarene commune in India! The only evangelists accepted in India are those proselytizing to the impoverished tribes and cyclone relief camps, where religion is traded for food-shelter-money. 'Get Aid with a free cross thrown in'.

But then Pappa Y is no evangelist. Pappa Y's commune is special. Very open, more liberal than one would expect. What do you expect from a Bene Israelite Jew born in India raised in the promised light and exiled from both? A tad impure in both lands. He separated from one, by his own volition, and his dad from their birthplace. Pappa Y – The father, the son, and the holy spirit of the commune. In the end – neither this nor that. There is a word in Indian mythology for his plight –*Trishanku*. Stuck crooning like Gerry

Rafferty. No surprise that Pappa Y wanted Willie to check out some ashrams in Pune for partnering with his Nazarene. They tend to be quite new-age too. He spent three decades in America, and God knows how many in Be'er Sheva prior to that, and yet had that aching for something Indian! As I said, you can take an Indian out of India but not India out of an Indian.

Willie traveled from New Haven all the way to Pune at Pappa Y's urging. He was so excited about his first visit to India and the ashram too. Though it was for work, I tagged along. He wanted me to. The plan was that I show him a bit of India, especially my hometown after a week in Pune. A wild week in Pune it was! Didn't inform Amma and Daddy – kept it hush-hush. A lot more was going on in some of these ashrams than just spirituality. A whole lot of swinging. My repressed prurience loved it – just for that week. Plus, Willie was very into Pappa Y back then. Not that Willie was ever part of the commune. No way would his Southerner parents ever have reconciled to that! He was just on a scholarship from Pappa Y's foundation – it's what funded his Master's degree.

After Pune, he tagged along with me to Udaipur. Willie was bewildered by the transformation in me. I slipped naturally into the Indian girl persona. I didn't even have to go to the changing room. It was more like I slipped back into my original identity. But he didn't see it that way. He wasn't familiar with that avatar of mine. Those were still early days. I felt all the allegiance an Indian feels to her motherland. With

Daada, Daadi and Naani, all the more. It is a generation thing. Even with Willie's grandparents in South Carolina, it's the same – a very different world. The occasional racial slur against African Americans slips out. Even if they are courteous to me and consider my Indian-ness different somehow. How? But after all, his grandparents did grow up before the civil-rights movement. And so it is with my Daada, Daadi, and Naani in India. Not the civil rights thing, but I guess the man-woman thing and the caste thing. The latter a bit muted, inspired by Gandhiji's influence on the urban educated class. Nevertheless, that generation had even more stringent expectations. It was evident in my behavior. I was docile, and apparently more 'exotic'. I didn't feel so, but Willie pointed it out to me later. Many months later.

You should have seen the look in his eyes. It was awe. It wasn't the shock from my transformation as I fitted into my role of a prankster-*saali* hiding the shoes of the groom at my cousin's wedding and everything else all of us cousins were conspiring about. It was not the wonderment of my traditional saris nor my mehandi (henna) all the way to my elbows. I am sure that played into his head too. He was just wonderstruck at the free radical playful girl haranguing the groom. What can I say? It was my right! After all these years, now I can see the exoticism in it all — the wedding rituals, a new dress for each ceremony every few hours. He was enamored by the deluge of colors in my dresses. I was celebrating my return to the colors of life. Honestly, I had been feeling rather color-deprived during the fifteen months at Yale. I overdosed on pastels and craved bright and bold. I think he was color-dazzled and thunderstruck.

My cousin Jagriti put it a little differently. "Aiiee, look at William ya! He is doting on you like a puppy!"

Not that I hadn't noticed. I was basking in it throughout the shrieks and cheers as we goaded Jiji, while she frantically groped around in the water bowl for the ring. The groom chivalrously pretended not to find it. Back then I found it charming. Back then I didn't know it was pretense. I am still not convinced. I don't expect men, any men to be so dexterous. Did he actually pretend? Or did he trick us into believing that he 'took a dive' as Will put it? A pretend pretend.

I was still enamored by the whole concept of a man. It was still that phase when they had just metamorphosed into a prospective and you start discovering the charming aspects of the brutes you have been dealing with through your childhood. Except it isn't societal like in Jane Austen's, it's purely hormonal.

His gaze of adulation from behind the sea of heads was exhilarating. It tickled its way from behind my neck into my temporal lobe. That feeling of a cold spray of pure awe from the showerhead of my frail-ego man's gleaming eyes. Thrilling. He wasn't yet my man then. It is then that the fluttering butterflies in my stomach took wings.

The butterflies almost overwhelmed my tummy — 18 months later. When he proposed to me. We already knew somewhere in our heads that we would be getting married. I mean we had talked about it so many times after the trip to India. But it was still an elephant in the room once he had moved in with me in the flat I shared with Aditi and Smriti. It only made sense as I was the first to get a job. We would hear the heaving sighs from the elephant's trunk whenever the future fluttered around between us after our lovemaking. We never talked about it. Now that I think of it, he was quick to descend into snores even back then. But then he did propose. It was around this time when he wanted us to join the Pappa Y's commune. Pappa Y had offered him a job, and we would have to join the Nazarene commune. Willie was crazy about the whole freedom-without-conditions thing. An unharnessed bull — as the village folk in India call it. And Nazarene was just that. I liked it in concept. But that's that. We live in a society and cannot go against the basic norms and morals that form the fabric of civilization. Every strand is connected with others to make up the fabric. We can't just run away. The fabric of society would rip. Fortunately, I persuaded him out of it.

"You can take your time finding your ideal gig," I assured him. But he was restless and would get fidgety every once in a while.

"A man should earn and provide." It once slipped out during a party half a year after our graduation. Half our friends were still unemployed. Scott, who I had dated briefly before Will, was drunk enough to suggest, "Hey Neeraja. How about having two lovers?

I am poor, you've made it big and we both know I love you too." He was joking. Drunk and joking. We were all a bit drunk. But that unnerved Will.

He started getting fidgety. "It is not right that I should be leeching off you." He was not! He still paid a bit of the rent and half the groceries. It was just his male ego – the collective unconscious of the Y chromosome.

He proposed to me in the city. In the broad dazzling lights of Broadway, by the Flat Iron. The whole shebang! And what a stone it was. He put all his first salary into it. That look on his face as he knelt in front of me, with everyone watching – the jaywalkers and the traffic. Not that any of them were watching. New Yorkers don't have time for anyone around them. But the notion of it. It was priceless. His eyes sparkled brighter than the stone.

I have never gone tired of that look. That look of mischief mixed in a cocktail of adoration and adulation. He would always wear it when I role-played Natasha the Russian bride to his Billy the Hillbilly Texan drawl.

He would say, "That mail-order bride Natasha's Russian drawl on your dusky skin can save so many rhinos and their horns sweetheart! It is the biggest aphrodisiac ever."

He still agrees on the dusky skin part but has turned tone-deaf to Natasha's cajoles and mumblings.

I tried it in the last weeks of the first lockdown to no avail. He was more interested in the freaky Tiger Show on Netflix. I soon gave up.

Trust me, it takes a lot out of me to put the Natasha accent on, after seeing him go days together in the sloppy 'You deserve a BJ!' T-shirt he got from his last visit to California. A T-shirt and boxers. Forever! His awkward knees are too angular to be pulling it off with any flair. He did seduce me in those once though. With those same bare angular knees and the ruddy body hair. In his dorm room twelve years ago. Long before I saw the more charming side of him in his jackets and suits and chic clothes I have been picking out for him ever since.

Why wouldn't he put his pants on those jackets on for the Zoom meeting? The man I have always taken as the paragon of integrity liked his cavorts of deception. Talk about schizophrenia!

True, I was the one who dragged him into a schizophrenic life. But that was still his choice. Moreover, the identity I switch between my Indian social network and our American one is not as severe as when visiting India. Agreed, I have never seen him that schizophrenic in the two social groups we shuttle between — one of them I dragged him into. For, in my Indian social network, Willie struts around very much in the same White avatar that he does with our other social group – the American one. My Indian friends wouldn't like it any other way — they would label him a fake otherwise. We Indians are rather snobbish about letting anyone else in into our world. I mean it's okay as a visitor, but most find it pretentious if he would get too Indian.

All this role-playing can be exhausting. Is that why Will jumped into his sloppy self during the lock-down? Is he tired of his groomed role? But for me, it is a big turn-off. And yet, I swallowed the Russian pill and slipped into my Natasha role. I had to. I was desperate to rev up our flagging sex life. The Corona scare has had quite an impact. I had hoped the lisping seductress Natasha would trigger Billy the Hillbilly in him. Yet another level of schizophrenia infecting our complex lives! His uncanny Texan drawl would definitely turn up the temperature.

"Hey check this out! You won't believe your eyes!" was his unlit response to my: "Hyello Billy — my Amyerikan Preenz."

Unfortunately, the TV remote in his hand did not assure me of the double entendre I had hoped for. But there was still a glimmer. Some exotic porn perhaps? He knew I was not into porn. But I would have given him some points for trying. Alas! The TV screen came alive with a blond sunburned Hick and a tiger in a cage.

That night I had my first bout of insomnia. My mind went on like a spooled tape, playing in a closed loop.

"Something needs to change."

While he was fast asleep, the annoying snores from his big head drilled into my repose like a jackhammer. It was not just his big head that was limp and asleep.

And then there is this lack of imagination in his big head. He may nurse his fantasies for the little one, but in his big head, he just won't entertain anything. Where did all his favorite Guru — Pappa Y's philosophy disappear? Life being about Now — 'Dead yesterday, unborn tomorrow'. Vedanta? Yeah right! Those lines were straight out of Omar Khayyam's Rubaiyat. It was not that I was fascinated by his teachings back then; I was in love with everything that Willie was into. You know that early phase of romance when we tend to dote on everything our partners are fond of.

'Focus on the Now.'

I was down with it. Thinking about Mika's high school — still four years away gets me nervous. Diverting back to the present would definitely help.

But if we don't keep an eye on the future, and a perspective on past events, we can be blindsided by the present. What about the road not taken? How will we learn about ourselves? And take an inventory of where it has landed us in today's reality. If not about what we could've done differently. How will we prepare for the future we are leading ourselves into?

"Willie, can you imagine how we would've been if you had accepted Pappa Y's offer ten years ago?" I ask him. It is just a leisurely reflection while languishing in bed after some of our early morning exertions. Alas! The luxury from the pre-pandemic days.

"You mean if we hadn't gotten married and instead joined the commune?" Will inquires.

"Yeah, we wouldn't have had this mortgage. I wouldn't have to make my depressing ALS patient forums. You wouldn't have to deal with Kevin." Kevin is Will's boss — a narcissist who uses Will's hard work for his career leaps. And my quarterly meetings with ALS Patient Groups for our company's drug portfolio are not the highlight of my trips — their desperate condition depresses me.

Will has a different perspective.

"When has the mortgage ever bothered us?! C'mon, you like your travel every quarter! Getting away from the kids for a few days. All the reward points and miles you are collecting. Aren't you happy with all the jumps you've been making in your career? I have no complaints with mine".

He does love his business trips — me less so. He is projecting through me.

I counter.

"Yeah, but our life would've been so much simpler without this pressure to have more and more, acquiring new things that the Jacksons have rarely reviewed and Alis have recently bought." This part of Upstate New York was finally gentrifying. Rhinebeck's fixer-uppers were all converted to three-car garage family homes — and owned by mixed-race families. Rhinebeck!

Why was I rooting for his silly commune living fantasy then? Ten years too late and thank God for that!

He turned towards me but his eyes stared right through me, momentarily diverted towards the imagination I planted in his head.

"No poolside barbecues with Heiner, the Schwarzkopfs, and Sharmas every month? I don't think I can live without that, baby."

"I mean back then we did not know we'd have all this. We could've taken that path and would've never faced all this."

"Babe! I thought you were the one who persuaded me against the commune. Why would you regret that?" he said searchingly.

"Don't Babe me!" I snarl at him. He has that tendency. He resorts to calling me Baby or Babe to get his comeuppance.

He grunts. It's supposed to be an apology.

"I am not regretting it — just speculating, how that could've gone..." I optimistically persist, knowing too well how this conversation will end.

"Ennhhh!" he grunts, "Cuda, wuda, shuda." As he always does, never letting his imagination challenge the perception of how the future can look. Let it be a surprise!

Maybe, it isn't a bad idea, after all, to let the future just appear — to let my decision spring a surprise to him. Isn't that how he wants to play life?

And yet, I dread the day I would drop the bomb on him. Didn't we talk about frail male egos? And that is what I dread the most.

How would I tell him that the spark was gone — something very obvious throughout this year. How could I broach the topic without hurting my poor Willie?! His willie would agree about the spark thing. I have seen his limpid resistance to my fondles. But my Willie would still not agree. He would look for something to blame it on.

"I always knew Stella would put stupid ideas into your head." Now that poor Stella was anyway maligned everywhere for coming out with her abuse allegations — against his candidate for the election. Luckily everything else prevailed and his Senator still won. God knows what it would have been if things went differently in the elections. Willie can get bitter when he is hurt.

It's not true though. Stella would never try to put a cleaver between us. She, with all her cynicism toward men that comes from her traumatic past, tries to give me a dose of reality.

"It's not going to get any better with another man, Neeraja. Every man is the same but at least this one is crazy about you. Hold onto him," she has always said.

I decided to push out my decision by a week and had frantic calls with Shannon, Riya, and Aditi. We all brainstormed. They all finally agreed with me. Aditi eventually chimed in, after Riya gave her a spiel about divorce not being the end of love but rather an evolution of it — a better life apart. They all agreed that it should at least start with a separation subsequently leading to a divorce. The question was how. More importantly, how to get Will to see it not as an affront.

I suggested a date night — to celebrate the end of the worst days of lockdown and pandemic.

"Time to talk some things over."

I didn't want to get his hopes up too much on the 'date' part of the evening. That was Riya's suggestion.

He pulled me to him and kissed me like he hadn't in a few years. His teeth gently biting into my lower lip, tugging at it. My butt felt so comfortable in his firm hold. As if they always belonged there.

What was I doing? Did I make the wrong decision? Should I just call it off and stick to the date night instead? Maybe we could rekindle things. Now that we were getting into the routine of working out of home and reconciling to this new way of life. I wasn't scared but let's face it. This virus was not going anywhere, we needed to come to terms with it and the life it implied. Thoughts raced through my mind, as I felt his warm familiar palms kneading my derrière.

But do I want Mika and Mohini pulled into chants of "we want our freedom back"? Where else would it stretch? "I don't want the government telling me what vaccinations my daughters should be taking." The safety and health of my daughters put at the mercy of this individualist.

"Why should the government insist we vaccinate? Shouldn't an individual have the choice over their body? Isn't it what we are fighting for in being pro-choice in abortion? How is it any different? Why should they decide on what we medicate the kids with?! Shouldn't it be the parents' choice?!" He is constantly countering.

"Because we stop the spread of this pandemic, Willie," I would counter. "It is for that greater good. As a part of the community."

"But the kids?!" He would get indignant.

"It takes a village to raise a child, Willie. These are my kids — my decision is selfish. They are the future of this community, not just your heirs," I would get upset at his choice of argument.

"I don't even trust these new types of vaccines. How much have they tested them? They rushed them through. Hardly the quality control and efficacy one could expect. And by the way, none of them were even tested on children," he would counter my counter.

"Efficacy is a lot more complicated to calculate than the way you put it, Willie." He doesn't even know the rigor that vaccines go through in their testing and effectiveness in order to get approved. He just doesn't trust the government to make the decision for him. And for that, he will go to any lengths to throw dirt on the vaccine testing regime or anything else to see what sticks.

Did I really want that? The thought of the girls being raised with exaggerated awe towards individual freedom and a callous attitude towards the community, society, civilization, and life as a continuum rather than each life to itself, if they survive this ghastly pandemic without being inoculated by their anarchist father was enough inspiration to say it out loud right here and not even wait for the dinner date.

He smiled, his lips still on my lips. "I like the idea of a night out to ourselves, Babe! But let's push the date part of the night a few weeks away? Let's make it an evening to talk things over?" His inquiring gaze searched deep into my eyes to see if I was shocked or worried. He only saw relief in my eyes.

Did we have the same agenda in mind? Was he gravitating towards divorce as well? Is that what he meant by 'let's talk things over'? We knew each other so well!

But wait. Why would he be looking for divorce? What complaints did he have on me? I was trying hard to bring our passion back! Why would he blame me for the lost spark? Or did he not miss the spark?

Did he find a spark somewhere else? Is that why he wasn't his libidinous self anymore? But then I reined in my thoughts that were hurtling into a fissile chain reaction.

"Don't be silly, Neeraja," I calmed myself. "That is one thing you needn't be worried about — his being unfaithful". Oh great! Now I am talking to myself in the second person??! Still better than Julius Caesar I suppose.

It is not that I am blindly in love with Willie or blindly in love with the idea of being in love. If anything, Stella's scarred view on men and relationships has gifted me with a 6/6 vision of relationships — not to put anything beyond a man when it came to sexual fidelity. But given the situation of the pandemic and the lockdown, there was little room for a sneaky getaway, deceit, lying, and cheating. His lying or excuses to get away were definitely not on my list of complaints. Nor his absence away from home. Au Contraire!

If anything, I should be happy that we were both heading towards a similar conclusion. Shouldn't I be happy about it? That Willie and I agreed even on the fate of our marriage? What could be more satisfying than a mutually agreed separation! No heart breaks or bitterness and no one hurt.

I decided not to get ahead of myself. It was pointless to second guess what Willie wanted out of his 'talk things over'. All it meant was that things may be moving in the right direction.

I was relieved. I could finally dismiss my fervent prayers to ship me away from this reality into a new one. I didn't wish for a new birth, a new reality. I was ready to face this one. I started looking forward to the dinner.

II

SERMONS ABOUT THE UNSAID

"There is no such thing as reincarnation!"

Pappa Y starts with his shocker headline of the day in his distinctive Indian accent, heavy and rustic, and then gives a meaningful pause — for effect.

Today's sermon is supposed to be about 'The road not taken'. Not as a critique of Frost's poem or a discussion about the poem itself. But sure, the thought behind could have been that. It is Samar, Papa Y's favorite pupil these days, who brought it up during one of his sermons a few weeks ago. Samar has a penchant for literature. Perhaps she has been reading the poem 'The Road Not Taken' or perhaps it is just her afterthought from a missed opportunity that she regretted, having chosen a path in one of the many tantalizing crossroads that life brings us to. And yet Pappa Y, in his usual flourish, diverges asymptotically from the subject of today's sermon.

"This whole thing about the cycle of birth and death? It's nonsense! Being born again and then again, and then again, till you get it right, until Nirvana. Ludicrous!"

"It is just the sacred texts trying to give you hope. They fool you into believing there is always a next time."

"What is next time?!"

His dark eyeballs survey his audience, a throng of multiple colors of eyes, all glassed in veneration, as he starts his salvo of deliberate, weighted pauses.

"What is Time??!"

Another meaningful pause.

"There isn't a next time. The 'next' is only in our minds. Our minds trick us into feeling time as it glides past towards the future. Only in one direction."

And then he digresses further, into his parables.

"There was once a boy in Damascus — Muammar. And his mother would send him daily to the Souq to buy groceries. You know, sesame, parsley, dates, olives. And on his way, he would pass this maze of alleys."

"Every day... Usually taking his friend Rafiq with him."

Another of his pauses — this time a long one.

"He starts late today. Quite late. His Ammi was waiting for her brother – Muammar's loving uncle – to arrive from Jerusalem. His uncle would bring him gifts, toys, and *halwa*. He would be waiting to be engrossed in the small puzzles that Uncle would throw at him, before Uncle would veer off into grown-up conversations with Ammi. His Ammi would interrupt her engrossed chats with her brother about their family in Jerusalem. 'Muammar! Stop playing with the toys. Get to the Souq. I need fresh parsley and olives.' And he would scamper off to fetch Rafiq and head to the old town."

Another long pause, as the audience pulsates.

"His Uncle never came."

He rotates both his palms in negation.

"They kept waiting for two, three, and four hours and there was no sign of Uncle. And that is why Muammar is late for the Souq."

"But why didn't the Uncle arrive?" Rudi from somewhere in the audience asks.

Pappa Y frowns.

"That is beside the point. It is irrelevant why."

He dismisses away the question with an impatient gesture.

"But then Muammar does set off to the Souq taking Rafiq with him, a few hours late.

He trudges through the alleyways of the old town, weaving through the narrow alleys, around people carrying on their business, chatting, loading, and unloading at all the shops and business that throng the alleyways of the old town, he stops short in front of the Kohl salon!"

"He turns to Rafiq,

'I've been here. I've seen this before!'

He seems surprised and bewildered about it. Rafiq isn't. They both had been there before! Innumerable times! It is their daily routine. These two young boys had traversed the course through the maze of a Souq countless times since they were young kids."

So, Muammar hurriedly explains, detecting Rafiq's confusion.

'I don't mean yesterday or when we were younger. Not that way.'

"But he was very sure of what he said to Rafiq next.

'Today. Now! I know I have been here like this, but not this now.'

A light flashes in Muammar's eyes as he deftly changes gears.

'By the corner, at the food shop, by the big roll of Lehem, we'll see Zahir. He is wearing a Kufiyah with the Agal. And he'll be talking to Bilal — the Frankincense trader from Salalah.'

"Rafiq looks at him quizzically. Traders in Damascus seldom wear Kufiyah with an agal. Zahir almost certainly never did. What was the occasion?"

Papa Y pauses, a playful smile, the white streak of his teeth appears between his thick dark mustache merging into his long beard. His audience is dying to turn around the corner into the other courtyard of the Souq, where Zahir's Shawarma shop heats up the alleyway.

"And indeed in a minute, they came across the old man Zahir in his shop wearing a Kufiyah with an agal. And indeed, in conversation with him is a man with a strong Yemeni accent. The whole corner is smelling of the strong scent of incense from his clothes! People in this part often confuse Salalah to be in Yemen."

And again Papa Y digresses into the details of the Arabic culture and perceptions.

He beckons Samar, his favorite disciple off late.

"Samar, my fellow exile! Both betrayed by our home!"

Only he, despite being a Jew — albeit a bene-Israeli — can get away by calling a Palestinian girl of Samar's stature his fellow exile.

And Samar deftly folds Pappa's shawl — coincidentally a white and red checkered woolen one that he pulls out of nowhere like a rabbit out of a hat — into a Kufiyah around her head.

And then as she finishes working on it, he announces her and the Kufiyah with a flourish of his arms.

He switches back to his parable, as he pulls her down to seat her next to him in a lotus position, tight in the embrace of his left arm. Samar sports a triumphant smile ear-to-ear.

"Muammar is very sure it is not some yesterday or the year before he is talking about.

'It is some other time not like this and I am not the same. I cannot even see I am me, but I just know that it happened.'

Poor Muammar is struggling to explain it."

"Dé-jà-vu!"

He announces proudly.

It is the sense of dé-jà-vu Muammar was having. We all have it in our lives. But Muammar could not explain it.

He pauses again.

"He is not as eloquent in his French."

There is a scattered peal of laughter from those in the awed audience who get his offbeat humor. A streak of white peers through the thicket of his dark mustache and beard again. He lets his smile linger too.

"Dé-jà-vu."

He chews the French phrase for emphasis and then pauses to add intrigue to it. There is pin-drop silence in the audience.

"Because Muammar is not lying. He is too young to be dishonest about this mundane bit. He feels he has been there because he has been there."

A meaningful pause, as the audience is in the firm hypnosis of Pappa Y's eloquence.

"The consciousness is the same, but the reality is different — interacting with the current you."

He usually locks his eyes, at this juncture, with someone in the audience who most relates to what he is saying. He has this way. He reads people's minds and zeroes in on those who have a similar story to tell. He knows!

The long pause gets the audience stirring at the gravity of what he's about to say.

"What Muammar felt was not the past or the future, but he did predict the immediate future!

It was that other time, that we call next time in rebirth.

There is no next time. It was just the other time. Maybe more than just one other time. Maybe many, many, many other times."

He makes these gesticulations with his hands, his long arms flailing wildly. And somehow he makes it come across that there are many instances of Zahir sitting by the Shawarma roll. "Other times."

"It was not in the past. But Muammar refers to it as the past. 'I have been here. But not as me. I cannot explain.' He could not explain it as a parallel event. Because if he knew it, it must be from before. It was his perception of time.

"We all perceive time to be linear. From past to future. Because our conscious mind is limited in its faculties. Because time is limited in the way it manifests itself to consciousness."

There is a rustle as his words start taking effect in people's minds.

"In our lives, we come across crossroads. It is at such crossroads that we create other incarnations of ourselves. By taking the road not taken. Every path on that crossroad, every road not taken has been taken by us. Creating some other version of us. And have become other births for us. And not necessarily in the past. They may be happening right now!"

A long pause for effect, as he waves his arms around.

"Mysteries of the Universe!"

They gasp it out aloud with him. He raises his arm in finality, a conductor imitating the slow rumble of the drums.

"The road not taken!"

He turns to Samar, nodding to her. Her dark eyes lined in kohl, wide in their whiteness like two fish swimming on the waves of her cheekbones, smile in gratitude.

He hadn't forgotten what the sermon was about.

"The road not taken."

He repeats it as if to underline the theme.

Pappa Y locks his eyes with Rudi as if he is answering him.

Rudi eagerly quizzes back.

"But Pappa Y, Muammar had no choice in that. Every time we are at crossroads, we have a choice of which road we will take and which road we will not.

Muammar did not have a choice. Why would he have a sense of de-ja-vu?"

Pappa Y strokes his beard and smiles patiently.

"Maybe his uncle did."

Britta snaps her fingers. She is always the smartest one around.

"Maybe Muammar is just a victim of his Uncle's choice of whether he would come to visit Muammar's Ammi."

Pappa Y smiles approvingly.

Britta encouraged, speculates, "Maybe Muammar's uncle had the choice to take the bus to Damascus or postpone it to another Friday. Maybe his Uncle stood at the crossroads about to walk to the bus station in Jerusalem. Something tempted him away."

"His mistress," someone from the back of the audience cackles.

Pappa Y laughs in unison but raises his index finger.

"Hold on, who is that clairvoyant in the room?! I am genuinely impressed! For a man's intransigence to familial duties, there is always a temptation involved."

Britta continues, "He encounters his mistress on the way?"

Pappa Y nods somberly.

Encouraged, Britta builds on her speculation.

"She is young and beautiful. That is the Uncle's temptation. She invites him over, 'My husband is out of town, it is new moon today — too dark for neighbors to police the street'. The horny Uncle is tempted."

Pappa Y nods approvingly again.

Britta beams and concludes, "The horny Uncle turned towards the pretty girl's house and chose that road."

The audience stirs, some giggle, and others use the pause to ease up.

Pappa Y explains,

"Who knows? The Uncle could've had more self-control? And politely decline. 'Some other day my love'. Who knows?!"

Samar queries,

"Pappa Y! What if the road was determined even earlier, when the girl's husband decided at the last minute NOT to go out of town, leaving the Uncle no choice but to take the road to head to Damascus"

Pappa Y ardently motions his hands towards Samar.

"That could as well be. And if it could, it did!"

Samar loves finishing Pappa Y's sentences. "And that would again lead to some new reality, some other parallel universe."

Encouraged, Britta continues with her framing of the whole parable to its conclusion.

"And in a reality where the Uncle resisted the temptation and did head to Damascus to meet his sister, Muammar would've been savoring the *halwa* his Uncle brought from Jerusalem, solved a few puzzles till his Ammi hollered at him to bring parsley and olives from the Souq."

Eager to show her bit, Samar chimes in, "And despite these distractions, Muammar was still earlier than the three hours delay to the Souq. He would've run to the Souq and in his hurry, forgotten to take Rafiq with him."

And Britta concludes in her breezy certainty, "And that would've been the Muammar who arrived at the Souq a few moments earlier to witness Zahir in conversation with the Frankincense trader from Yemen."

Pappa Y corrects Britta immediately, "Salalah, not Yemen."

He looks at his audience,

"Could've...Would've...."

And he lets the audience finish it for him.

"Should've!" In a loud cheery finish.

He gestures his right hand as if he is conducting a short piece of some ensemble with an invisible baton.

"There is no could've, would've, should've.

There are no roads NOT taken. Every road at the crossroad is taken."

Pappa Y locks his eyes with Stella who is sitting in the front row, right below where his couch is. She nods a very knowing smile. A nod of seeing it all. She gets it. So he smiles. As if sharing some clandestine secret.

"In Fundamental Physics, they call it Multiverses. Parallel Universes. They think there are other universes that ended up differently after the Big Bang. Maybe they did. Maybe they keep getting created after every such crossroad! Or maybe there is only a finite set of those, all predestined, limited by the stochastic feasibility of permutations and combinations."

"But Pappa Y!, where are all those other Universes?" Britta enquires.

He turns to Britta, his trusted right hand since Mary left Nazarene for her villas at Saintes-Maries-de-la-Mer in France along with Magda.

He pivots both his hands into a perfect clockwork-up, his brow knotted quizzically.

"If I give you the answer my love, they will call me to Stockholm. Pappa Y will be the next Nobel Prize Laureate in Physics."

He pauses for the laughter to settle down. He smiles at Britta enquiringly.

"Maybe you can do the math for all that, Britta. Like those two professors in Zürich who did it for Einstein. We can both get our Nobel Prize and be famous."

Britta smiles back, her eyes twinkling. She knows she is the brains of the Nazarene commune these days. Since Joshua's exit from Nazarene after the tragic Trial.

"They speculate those other Universes can be accessed through blackholes that lead to white holes or wormholes. Who knows?!

But those other universes are not hidden in some interstellar wasteland. We feel them during our dé-jà-vu."

And those are the Pappa Y metaphysical reflections that have made his Nazarene commune what it is.

Britta pulls some of the confused pupils into a corner as the gathering in the Mandala Hall begins to disperse. If the Nazarene commune were a lifelong university, Pappa Y the professor, Britta would be his research assistant giving the after-class tutorials.

"And each road taken leads to a different outcome, a different reality, and a different life. In your life, in your reality, you think of this road not taken. But you, not the same you but of the same consciousness, have taken the other road and your current road that had led you to Pappa Y — as the road not taken."

III

HE SAID WHO SAID? — WILLIE
(William Joseph Babbitt)

It was a bizarre dinner. And that too considering it was just Neeraja and me! Something was seriously amiss. How can anything with my one true love ever get bizarre?

It started out like every dinner date between us; there were more empty tables at the restaurant but that could be the pandemic that kept most people at home stuck in their irrational paranoia.

The State Street Bistro Chèz Pierre was cozy and classy, the way it has always been the last 10 years since we stumbled onto it. Pierre greeted us with his usual affable thick French accent. No surprises there. Neera ordered an Alsatian Gewürztraminer and I stuck to my Paso Robles Cabernet Sauvignon. No surprises there as well. It is there that my nationalism begins and ends — with my love for Californian Cabernet. Supporting neighborhood businesses is my motto (something that Pappa Y strongly advocates throughout the Nazarene commune).

Neeraja ordered a Chicken Tagine — always with that lurking guilt for the chicken. I mean get over it! It's chicken! In some cultures, it is not even considered meat. But even that, she prefers laced with Moroccan spices — not as much as Indians drown theirs.

"The spices will hide the off taste of meat," she always justifies.

"What meat?" I always joke. "Chicken?! At least order some duck!" I usually urge her.

I feel that little bit of guilt in her heart and I try to numb it with my playful taunts. I think it's very gutsy of her to have switched to meat, considering that she was raised a vegetarian.

"No one has eaten meat in my family in the last fifteen hundred years," she proudly boasts.

"How can you be sure?" I usually challenge her.

"True," she grudgingly admits. That lost look that knots her eyes in doubt — it's cute.

"My cheating genes must be coming from some cheater up the line," she quips back. "I feel very close to him, whoever he was," she adds icily. There is that lilt in her giggle. Drives me crazy. She still has that effect on me.

"Why do you think it is one of your great Grandpas? Why not a great Grandma?" I start needling her.

She would roll her eyes, "Indian women stick to legacies and heritage more than men. We carry the responsibility of human heritage you know!" she announces. I am not sure how proud she is about it.

But seriously, coming from a tradition of just eating vegetables and dairy and then one day, boom, switching to meat just because the man she loves is such a meat-eater? Would I switch to dog meat if my girlfriend had been from Guangdong or Korea? No way!

I almost died of starvation those two weeks at her parent's place in India eleven years ago. Pure vegetarian everything for two weeks straight, except when I went out with Neera to restaurants. But that was maybe two or three times max.

And then there was Satya Prakash Kashyap (what a mouthful!) — SP, her Dad. Always bare-chested when at home, wearing a string thing across his torso. Not too different from my Pa with his pants unbuttoned during dinners. It was even more hilarious seeing SP pull that thread around his ears every time he went to the John.

"It's a Brahmin tradition. We must pull our baptism thread around our ear when we answer nature's call," he would educate me in his thick Indian accent. He's a cool guy. So fluent in English, despite his accent. Very Shakespearian though.

"Why are you staying for only a fortnight?" he asked me back then.

"Fortnight??! Where are we? Stratford by Avon?!" I joked with Neera later. It was long before the video game came out. Now Mika is more familiar with the word, although she has no clue of its history or how the actual word used to be spelled. Mika's rather good at the game though.

It was those ancient Brahmin traditions that hit me hard during that visit. He would mumble a prayer, sprinkle water around his lunch, and slurp some drops of water from his right palm. Not too different from my parents' prayers at every meal — insistent on thanking the Lord for the food on the table. Every meal! C'mon!

Fortunately, neither Neera nor I take to our traditions. Neither my prayers nor her wearing the thread across the torso. The thread would look funny across her boobs. Like a sexy topless Bolivian guerrilla sporting a bandolier. Except a belt of bullets between her breasts would become a new fetish for me — much better than a strand of yellow thread. I fantasize about her pulling that imaginary sacred bandolier around her ear whenever she hits the John.

"Women don't get baptized as Brahmins," she corrects me in her melodious allure. But it does tickle her.

It was during that 'fortnight' that I fell in love with Neera. A month actually. We had spent a week in Pune earlier and another week later at her cousin's wedding. What a spectacle it was! I always had a thing for her. Her dark exotic skin, jet-black hair, and large, intriguing eyes had captured my being when I first met her at business school a year earlier. And we were already kind of dating. But the cousin's wedding was pure magic!

I have great memories of the two weeks at her parent's house despite the overdose of vegetarian food. It was spicy but I was already developing quite a palate for my spice tolerance — Indian or Thai. I can now beat any man with hair on his chest at that game. Jalapeños, Thai pepper, Piri Piri, or even Habanero! Bring it on!

Although, I still can't imagine what it would be for her parents if the roles would reverse. And I was playing the host to them. A pure meat diet for two weeks cooked by yours truly?! What would they eat?

Oh well... Cuda wuda shuda.

Pierre did a great job with my beef entrecôte, but something didn't feel quite right. Not the food — the aura of the evening was bizarre. I ordered it rare and the sight of Neera's eyes popping out when it arrived. Holy cow! She has those adorable doe-like eyes. Dark eyes shaded by beautiful jet-black crescent brows that make her so sumptuously beautiful. Vegetarian or Vegetarian-lite. Who cares?!

"And these are the lips you love kissing, sweetheart." I have always teased her when she brings up her reservations about red meat. She says it is bad for the heart and a huge burden on the environment. But give me a break! It is about the cow and it being holy in her religion. She claims it is not holy. That the cow is regarded as a mother figure. She is not religious about it anymore though. But she still does practice a few rituals here and there.

Pappa Y insists on that.

"Never deny the traditions of your heritage. They form the undercurrent of your subconscious."

She is raising her daughters Mika and Mohini with some exposure to Hindu traditions. I am all for it. I shouldn't be calling them 'her' daughters, my adorable kittens! I am supposed to be their biological father. I am sure of Mika. She exhibits the same chutzpah. So many things about her, I feel it is me but in girl form. If I had been emotional, girly, quick-to-tears, soft, and sporting pink as a child, that would be Mika. She fulfills my dreams of being a father that no son ever can. Why would I have a son? I knew what an asshole I was growing up.

But who am I kidding? I adore Mohini more! But Mohini as my daughter, the jury is still out on that. Neera insists she is. And who am I to question that? I still tease her though and she just rolls her eyes. I am glad she doesn't take it personally. That I am accusing her of lying or something. I am not.

Moreover, tiny Mohini is nothing like me. But I can't live without her. I mean in addition to Mika. I am Mohini's favorite too. Rudi doesn't even come a close second to me.

It is Rudi whom I suspect is her biological father. I say it because of the time he spends with Neera. And I can see she digs his intellectual side. He is a brainiac, a

Doctorate in Quantum Physics. And that is why I think Mohini is Rudi's seed. She is so smart. She could never have gotten that from me. But she is an extrovert — none of his introversion, softness, or clumsiness. She is actually quite athletic. Whizzes past like a bullet. Never walks, always bounds. I think she is a lot like her mom in that way.

A man's instinct can't be wrong though. And then it is said that humans are the closest genetically to Rhesus monkeys and baboons. In Rhesus monkeys, every baby in the tribe exhibits external traits of the biological father in early childhood. That's nature's way of protecting the baby from the extreme jealousy of the male monkeys. And Mohini never looked like me even as a baby. But I wasn't a Rhesus monkey when she was born. I took her into my hands. She was so tiny. I couldn't have spotted the difference. But then Britta put it into my head one day. "Mohini doesn't look like you at all," she said. How could she tell from that tiny face?

She put that doubt into me. And now when I do suspect it and tease Neera about it, she is quick to lecture me.

"We mostly know when we conceive. Our intuition just tells us. I can tell you when she was conceived — when we were making love under that gazebo, during that thunderstorm remember?" Neera points to the beautiful stretch under the gazebo in the park by the Mandala Hall.

I remember that evening quite well. Little over three years ago. It was raining hard. We were drenched. Neera mentioned something about the Bollywood movies from her childhood and the love-making innuendoes in rainy song sequences. It was then that she had dragged me to the gazebo. She loves the notion of being observed when we have sex. She is a closet exhibitionist. We have so much of it. I bet she doesn't get that with Rudi. I never asked her. Not that I am jealous. I am just happy that I still mean as much to her. I am just content with that look she has whenever we meet. Dinner date or not.

But not this dinner date.

The look in her eyes, as we finished our dessert, my heart did skip a beat. That was where the dinner got bizarre. I had this feeling that she was going to say something terrible. Her eyes were searching deep into my eyes to see if I had the strength in me to take it.

Take what?!

The portent of it pushed my heart into a deep dive. I was draining the last of my Sambuca — munching the coffee bean, when she said, "I think we need to get divorced."

I don't think she started with that sentence. She must've started with something before she came to that sentence. She must've started about Mika and Mohini and something about it not being fair on them or something like that.

"I don't want them growing up with a Dad who teaches them 'to each his own' and the radical idea of individual freedom without social responsibility."

I don't remember all of what she said.

Who remembers every sentence of a dream?

It is just the mood of the dream that riddles us during and after the dream. And it was those words 'divorce' that stuck in my head and pulled the dark sock onto my head.

****

I woke up with a start. It was still dark in Britta's bedroom. She was still curled up against me — her thigh around my waist. She stirred, opening her eyes, regarding me with her myopic eyes. She always takes her contacts off before we make love.

Her soft palm was immediately on my bare back. It felt warm and reassuring. There was something about Britta. So sure and so poised. So very reassuringly mature.

"A bad dream?" she inquired in a calm and comforting voice. It brought peace back to me. I looked at her, over the bare round of her seductive shoulder and nodded. Her warm hands continued stroking my back. My breath was still a bit rushed as she continued massaging.

"Sleep here tonight. You'll feel better," she suggested. I agreed and went back to sleep. Britta's warm assuring skin by my side calmed me.

I got up early the next morning, still wondering about my bizarre dream, still reeling under the stab of guilt. I gave Britta a grateful long kiss all over her bare back racing down like an alpine piste, as she moaned softly. As I tiptoed out of the bedroom she mumbled, "We'll talk about your dream later, OK." And drifted back into her tango with Somnus, a smile curling onto her pretty face and pushing against her peachy cheeks. She was content that I spent the night in her bed.

What did she see in me?

"It's always good to admire and love what one doesn't have in oneself," she quips. Even her sarcasm is so incisive. And then she calmly adds, tongue in cheek, "Your gregarious sparkle completes my sullenness" dissecting our mutual attraction with such lofty words. I always raise one eyebrow in cockiness. It pits me against the legendary Joshua of Nazarene whom she openly admits as her one and only complete love — the one she could never have.

"Get over yourself! You are still in the top 25 percentile," she jokes. She is not a woman of many words. Even her smile as she slept, her auburn hair falling over her cheek was brief and terse in its gratification. Women are strange that way, they sleep so blissfully with someone next to them. Men do not share the same enthusiasm for company. We sleep a lot better in an empty bed. Perhaps I should not generalize.

I walked back to my cottage and jumped into the shower to wash off any remnants of the queasy dream.

Later in the day, that afternoon, after our meditation at the Commune's Lotus Meditation Hall, I ran into Neera as she stood chatting with Rudi, in no hurry to roll up their yoga mats. Her face nodded animatedly as Rudi went on with his didactic monologues.

She felt me approaching and turned to me, her crescent brows immediately knitting into the two sides of a baseless triangle, the knotted apex cutting into the furrow of her forehead.

"Why the long face Will?" she perceives my moods so well.

I kept silent. Honestly, that acerbic hole in my stomach from the night before was still searing my insides. My soul had turned itself inside out, trapping my chattiness in its invisible loop.

"Seriously dude." Rudi slapped my back. "Why so quiet? We want you at your yappy best at the symposium tomorrow. At your speaking best — not this sullen hermit that Britta is trying to make you." A nervous giggle. He could never pull off a cackle even if he tried.

"Had a terrible dream," I confessed to Neera. If her countenance was knotted earlier, it was brimming with worry now.

"What kinda dream?" she sighed, fearing the worst, as she drew towards me.

"Alright, I'll leave you lovebirds alone." Rudi rolled up his yoga mat. "Neerja! Work on Will. He's gotta be in top shape for tomorrow. He's the best speaker we have." And he left.

Neera was still peering at me, her eyebrows knit together. She looked so adorable, I felt like kissing her. And I did. I cradled her face in my palms and gave her a long lingering kiss, softly biting her lower lip.

"I thought you had a bad dream? If that's the result of it, more points to those dreams," she smiled mischievously. She saw me cringe at the mention of the dream and almost immediately her arms tightened around me. It felt good.

"What is it, honey?" Her voice was so soft, it could have calmed the most fidgety of chihuahuas.

"I dreamt that you were divorcing me." I shuddered.

She looked at me quizzically, her arms still around me, her eyes still a few inches away from mine, her breath soothing my nervous nose.

And then she splintered into a peal of laughter. If her voice hadn't been so melodious, her pitch not so soothing, I would have said she broke into a guffaw. But she is too cute and too delicious to be guffawing.

"I did what?!" Mirth and amusement were brimming in her eyes. And it was so enchanting. It was like that evening at her cousin's wedding many many years back when I first fell in love with her. Her gleeful notes and the amusement in her eyes blew my gloom away into smithereens.

"It felt very real! It was as if we were married and those words you said plunged a dagger into me. It felt like the end of the world to me," I confessed, a bit whiny. I was enjoying her face so close to mine. I was trying to milk it.

She disengaged one of her arms and stroked my cheek, her fingers tracing my nose and my lips. "Don't worry sweetie-pie. How can I divorce you?! Not unless you want to get married and get us kicked out of Nazarene," she smirked.

Did I detect a twinge of regret in her voice or was it my imagination?

She looked into my eyes intently, as if she read my thoughts. "I never regret the day I quit my job and you took up Pappa Y's offer. I never liked my job that much anyway. Look how happy you are! So blissful, so free like an eagle gliding in the blue sky above. I wouldn't want my Willie any other way."

I tugged her toward me with my hands on the small of her back. "What about you hon?"

"I am always happy, my dear. This way or the other. And this way we have our Mika and Mohini." And she immediately mimed me, "I know, I know... what if Mohini is Rudi's seed?" She rolled her eyes, and said, "Someday you'll know it from inside you." And then she squeezed my cheek fondly. At that moment I wished I was married to her. Just for that moment, I felt that all the exhilaration and ecstasy with Britta, Masha, Sheherza, Zhihua, and all the freedom the Nazarene commune has gifted me were not worth compared to having her as mine, and mine alone.

"Who knows what would have happened if we had gotten married? Would we have lasted this long? Who knows if we would have had Mika and Mohini then? Who knows? Perhaps we'd have two sons? Two assholes you'd play softball with," she teased me. "And for Daddy to be content in some perverse way of continuing the Kashyap family name, even though it wouldn't. And Amma to be thankful to her ancestral saints with no rational basis, always answerable to the glowering line of patriarchs long dead."

"Eeennhhh, cuda wuda shuda," I dismissed it. I remember the day Mika was born. In the same ward — 'The Barnyard Ward', where the legendary Joshua was born more than forty-five years ago. Everyone was celebrating.

Every birth in Nazarene is celebrated with a ceremony over which Pappa Y personally presides. All the men have the deceptive illusion of being the father. But the biological fatherhood can often, if not always, be an open secret. Pappa Y took the time to clink a glass with me. His knowing eyes smiled at me.

"Congratulations proud father! It is your wish come true, a daughter that the Universe has gifted you!"

I had hoped deep inside my heart that it would be a girl from that day fourteen years ago when Pappa Y had announced in the morning prayer hall that Neeraja was with child. She stood beside him, decked in ceremonial Indian clothes, bedecked with jewelry. Pappa Y had even invited some Indian priests from the Malibu temple and some womenfolk to the ceremony.

We get a flavor of every culture and tradition of the would-be mother at such ceremonies. She looked a lot more resplendent than at her cousin's wedding years before. True, she had lost her playfulness. True, she was no longer the most eligible girl that she said she was at that wedding. But that somehow added to her aura.

From the elevated stage where she stood with Pappa Y, Neera had stared right at me, as I stood lined up amongst all the menfolk as we applauded and cheered. Her eyes were gleaming and so very radiant, proud of gifting me exactly what I was dreaming of. And somehow Pappa Y had read into that dream of mine. As he does with everyone.

Neera continued caressing my nape with her palm, as I stood there watching more people drift off from the Lotus Yoga Hall. "The joy of having a baby is so exhilarating by itself, Willie, that it doesn't matter this way or that way to me. There are times, I wished Mika was a son, now that she is getting to that recalcitrant age."

Indians and their vocabulary! Why can't she just use ordinary words?

"I am glad Deidre and Jana are so much better at handling her teenage tantrums." She mumbled under her breath, "But there are more times when I am glad she isn't a boy!"

I gently stroked her butt. She has juicy hips, tight and full. She is so sexy and carries herself so well, in the choicest of dresses or naked. Although, Zhihua gets a few more points for her naked body. So slender, lissome, taut, and with such soft skin. And then there is Britta, who has maintained herself so well at her age. And the thought of all those naked women hosed away my gloom.

"Oooo! Someone is getting all riled up!" Neera giggled, as I pressed against her.

Yes, we couldn't ever get divorced. I was glad that we had not gone the marriage route that fateful day fifteen years ago.

****

She was lying naked atop me, gently tickling my earlobes with her tongue, as her breasts nestled my face. We had returned from our Graduation gala 40 hours ago, drunk, high, and in ecstasy. Or high on ecstasy, I couldn't tell one from the other. We were catching up on sleep after we found time and some food leftovers from the refrigerator. There was always food leftover in the apartment. Aditi, Neera's flatmate, a Computer Science graduate student at Yale, was an eager and amazing cook, and so was Smriti the other flatmate. The lost one we used to call her. Always seemed lost in some other world. I wonder where she has disappeared.

Neera was the worst of the three in her cooking but still did amazingly well.

"Do you think we will have the same fire in us after marriage Willie?" she had enquired, sketching indecipherable doodles on my face with her long locks.

"For the next thousand years, my eggplant angel," I whispered into her ears. She's more the color of Kiwi but that simile doesn't do any justice to her milky smooth skin.

The mist of all the mind-numbing substances of the last forty-eight hours cleared right there! Suddenly, an apparition of a robed bearded figure formed by the glare of the door, beyond the silhouette of Neera's twin butts. It was Pappa Y — the fabled Magi from across the dunes. And that reminded me of his job offer a few days ago. Was it my subconscious mind concocting it? Or was it all the leftovers in my bloodstream? Or was Pappa Y making one of his mystical appearances? He is known to eavesdrop on dreams and thoughts. There are legends about how he appeared in the dreams of none other than the Diva — Mimi. And she wasn't even ever part of Nazarene.

Should I be embarrassed that he was catching us in this state? Awe heck. He is no prude; he'd be proud of us. He would even suggest a few tantric tricks to spice it up. Plus, he has this soft corner for Indians. He was after all born a Bene Israeli Jew in India many many decades ago. I am sure he approved of my naked state of affairs with the Indian girl of my dreams. I approved of it and so he better.

"On second thoughts," I whispered languidly into Neera's ear, taking a cue from Pappa Y. A strand of her raven hair dancing above her soft ear to my voice,

"There is another way we can keep the fire burning between us for the next thousand years."

Pappa Y, his hands crossed as if he were a judge observing our act critically, lifted his right hand and made a sign.

"Way to segue, my man," it seemed to say. I wasn't so sure of how Neera felt. She partially lifted herself and strode me, her knees on the bed, her haunches pinning my waist. She regarded me with doubtful curiosity. 'Where is he going with this?' was her look.

She inspected me from head to chest, the rest of my body cowering under her hips, slightly uncomfortable at her glowering scrutiny.

It's not that I had never proposed to her. I don't know if she had nursed any dreams of that whole ritual of me on my knees and offering her the ring. I couldn't afford a stone worth her 'I do' anyway. I was a fresh grad, I was broke. My scholarship with Nazarene had finished with my graduation. Neera had already landed a job. Always the smarter one. We were contemplating moving into a new apartment. It would come to it sooner than later. I guess it was already a *fait acompli*.

Perhaps that is why my segue alarmed her. I thought it was a great transition. Pappa Y in my phantasmagoric mirage seemed to affirm. But then women have this uncanny intuition. It's almost as good as Pappa Y's clairvoyance. Or at least so it seemed.

I kissed her nipple that swung around my eyes tantalizing me. I don't know, I thought it would reassure her. It would reassure me if she did that. Pappa's stare hurried me on. I desperately searched for the next transition. A smooth landing. Not that there was anything to fear.

"Pappa Y has a job offer for me. But the offer is valid only…" I hurriedly ran iterations of phrases, "…for commune members."

There was a moment of pregnant silence as she strode on me, her glance penetrating me through my eyes into my brain. I had to come up with something that would release her clenched breath, as pretty as it made her upright breasts glowering at me interrogatively. And it slipped out fluidly straight from my heart, without any effort. Full candor.

"I will never take up the job offer without you."

"What do you mean?" her soft voice full of hope enquired, her chest already deflated, her pouting breasts a little farther away from my nose. Out of relief?

"We join the commune and I take the job. I ain't going anywhere without you. Anywhere." And that was the truth.

Pappa Y winked at me, a thumbs up, and disappeared.

"You always loved the concept of the Nazarene," I cajoled her.

She was silent. A long ominous silence. I curbed myself from getting ahead of myself. 'You gotta listen to your woman when you get that stare," my Old man seemed to be saying.

She pursed her lips, biting the lower one.

"I do...but..." her voice eased the strain of silence.

I forged ahead. "C'mon! You liked Pappa Y the one time you met him. You said he had immense spiritual strength." I gave her a little more time to let it sink.

"Silence is good sometimes," Pappa Y seemed to be whispering in my head. "Give her time to think." Now he was right beside me.

I let another long pause slip. She ruminated.

I fed her the good pieces "It will be great. We as part of that commune. It is one big family. Free, liberated from the judging, restricted world we are always complaining about."

We wouldn't be getting married, she knew that. Nazarene was one happy commune that did not believe in such puritanical contracts. Sex and love were not a monopoly or a duopoly per the Nazarene principles. It was what flowed between all human beings. She knew that.

Together in a very different way. Not the way she'd dreamed of from her childhood. Not together as the conventional world defines it. But Nazarene was nothing of what the regular world was transforming into — controlling, judging, a menu of checklist accomplishments, a cult of notional freedom with most of actual liberty taken away and with too many dos and don'ts from the government and society. Nazarene stood for all the good with none of the hypocrisies breathing down our neck. But then she had her aspirations about her life, shaped by her childhood in an Indian Brahmin middle-class family, full of aspirations, checklists, compliances, judgments, and the need for approval.

Compliance, for her, was the just way to sustenance. 'What are we without our community? Our society, where everyone leans on each other and trusts each other. Where we trade into compliances for the sustenance of our generation into the next and onto the next.' Those are the thoughts that run through her genes that trigger the spark across every synapse of her brain.

Ironically, Nazarene as a commune offered much of it in more honesty and integrity than the world today offered, except for being unconventional, letting freedom take wings, and therefore defying regular compliance, setting its own traditions of sustainability for humanity.

In Neera's view, back then the sustainability of life was possible at Nazarene only if it was not in direct conflict with conventional wisdom of society at large. That interconnected web of life was important for her. It still is. A lot of fuzzy stuff. Not as revolutionary as mine. I believe in survival of the fit through defiance of what was wrong, by the rightful exercise of free will. We both agreed that the principles of Nazarene were more akin to true happiness than the world we were living in. Environmentally, ecosystem wise and societally. The only point of contention was defiance vs compliance, revolution vs hope of evolution.

It took another few more months to resolve it and bring her to see the value of exercising free will. And that's how we moved to the wonderful sunny weather of rural Southern California in the foothills of Santa Ynez mountains into the Nazarene Commune. I became the Digital Marketing Manager for Nazarene Outreach, the domain of Mother Mary, the mother of the legendary Joshua, the first child of the commune.

And look where we stand today! As the whole world reels from the pandemic, hurrying to enforce draconian regulations and camps sneaked through the curtain of fear hysteria whipped up everywhere, the Nazarene Commune stands as an example! The only place with a non-elected leader that was acting in the long-term interest of his people. Not elected, but Pappa Y was selected by God.

"Let us not forget that the pathogens merely fulfill their role in this grand nature," he had reminded us. Without clamoring for vaccinations and forcefully inoculating every moving creature in the commune, he had summoned his council and taken up measures to protect the weak and vulnerable and let the virus sneak into the robust healthy members. Benign Invasion, he called it. It prepares the community to build its immunity. Herd immunity that suddenly has become a sacrilege to utter in the world outside.

"Do not be afraid of suffering! For suffering and death is part of the whole truth! They are part of life!" He prepared everyone. In the end, people who felt they needed prophylactics took it, and the weak and vulnerable were cajoled to protect themselves with the vaccination. Even if an imperfect one, it protected them. Enough of us had our bouts of infection and suffering, but it gave the kids their boost of immunity by just being around us. The earlier virus had nothing to do with the children. Now the later variants are coming — our herd immunity naturally acquired is giving the kids their protection. While it is not all hunky-dory, we are not living in a world divided in resentment pitted against each other. And then we have always been proud of our hygiene, safety, and health practices.

****

The cleaning team started cluttering into the Lotus Meditation Hall breaking our reverie.

"You ready for tomorrow?" Neera purred, rubbing my back as she felt me against her.

I winked.

She could report it back to Rudi. Rudi is always rooting for me. We are a good team at all conventions that Nazarene sponsored. His research is diligent, and my presentations are impeccable.

"Rudi said it's not on Zoom anymore? It's Santa Barbara?".

"Ah, you mean the Conference?" I floated back from my reverie.

And that brought Neera back in sync. "Oh, you mean that? Well, that sweetie, shall HAVE to be in Santa Barbara!" She smiled impishly.

"But for this one, I'll have to dress up. I hope it's not too warm," I grunted.

She giggled.

"What's up with this abhorrence to dressing up?" She caught my drift. She had occasionally dropped into my cottage during my online conferences with the corporate world over the last few months. I would be dressed in business formals, tie and all. But only waist above. Down under, only in my boxer shorts. I was taking advantage of the online video environment. No pants needed. Don't think she appreciated my attire.

But what else was I supposed to do? With the world outside in hysterical paranoia? Shut down as if the bubonic plague was let loose. Quarantining like the lepers in Molokai. Curbing everyone's freedom. We at the commune continued with our life as usual. We took our precautions. Our medical practice is the best in the state. We voluntarily underwent health checks every time anyone returned from downhill into Fillmore, Oxnard, or Santa Barbara. We had our infection rates for not following the state strictures of a lockdown. But nothing alarming. We treated everyone early without any stigma.

Pappa Y and the government relations had managed to fend off the Sheriff of Ventura County officials and their draconian rules, even though it is Los Angeles that is the hotspot, not Ventura County.

I couldn't have been happier serenading in my domain, pants down.

"Don't you think it's dishonest?" she had clicked her tongue once. It nevertheless amused her, the few times she visited my apartment. Neera has her preoccupations with the kids and with Vahana, one of the Commune elders and a famous designer she liked working with. There's a lot more to that old dog!

"He's Daddy's age!" she scandalously whispered to me during one of our regular evenings at the park with the kids. "I have to wrestle with my mind to get that thought out of my head when we are... you know..." so many years at Nazarene and still prudish about the sexual part. Putting sex into its proper shelf as just another chore. A more pleasurable chore but nevertheless, as Pappa Y says, a "chore of nature like breathing, eating, and drinking". Neera hooked up with Vahana alias neè Roman Aslam two years ago. I think it was during the Carnival time that they had hooked up. We celebrate it the Venetian way. Everyone in costumes and masks. She did not recognize him. Halfway through in her bed, the masks came off. They nevertheless continued. And now they still spend time a lot even outside her projects. She likes his wise influence on Mika and Mohini. I am glad the kids get that. In the absence of the role of grandparents in the current day civilization, I am glad we get that in as many ways as possible at Nazarene.

"Good luck with tomorrow's symposium! But don't forget our thing at the Santa Barbara beach." she gleamed as she pecked me on the cheek.

"Your ex-boss will be there" I informed her.

"At the beach?! Why?"

And I looked at her incredulously. Sometimes she can get so ditsy.

"Oh, you mean the conference. Yeah, Stella called me to tell me she will see you. She got stuck in California before the Lockdown. You must be overjoyed to add such a name to the attendee list," she teased me.

"I guess," I replied.

I wasn't a fan of Stella, even when Neera worked with Stella, her first year after University. Stella has this rather slutty personality. Very flirtatious! She would openly flirt with me, her protégé's boyfriend!

Plus she derailed the career of Senator Broderick by accusing him of abusing her as a minor. I was a big supporter of Senator Broderick. He was true presidential material.

Plus she put all these things into Neera's head. Not that it matters. If at all, all her stuff, ironically sealed it between me and Neera even more tightly.

Stella became a #MeToo star ever since she ruined Senator Broderick's chances in the Primary.

"Her presence will augur well for the conference," I saltily admitted. "She's an icon, a #MeToo star. Full points to her." I replied neither admitting nor denying. Neera likes her. She always thinks of Stella as her mentor.

During the first year after graduation, when Neera was working for her, she would remark, "There is something amiss. Stella has this traumatized cloud in her eyes, something about her past. But she won't speak about it."

It took Pappa Y to persuade Sylvia, Stella's mother, and a big name at the National level with the Democrats, to reconcile with Stella. Apparently, when the abuse took place many decades ago, Sylvia dissuaded Stella from complaining.

"How can you be sure it was him? It was dark. It was someone at Monocle. A lot of important people come there from Congress. Someone was trying to be a pig. That's what men do. It isn't worth reporting. Don't make a fuss about it," she had advised Stella back then.

"He is too important to the party. The repercussions will be grave. It will end my career," she had added.

Stella broke ties with her mother after that, till Pappa Y intervened. He confirmed Stella's charges with his psychic power. The only time I disagreed with Pappa. As if one can disagree with clairvoyance.

"She has more to her than meets the eye, my son!" Pappa Y revealed to me knowingly, soon after. "You should be thankful for what she means to Neeraja. It's a gift," he says paradoxically.

But why would I care? I have Neera and that's all I care about.

"Will you be OK presenting with a mask on at the symposium?" Neera enquires, she knows my resentments too well.

"I guess so," I regretfully confirmed. It is a California State regulation.

"Ridiculous," I continued. "How can they expunge individual rights and make such authoritarian rulings? Shouldn't they leave it to the wisdom and deference of individual discretion? Feed the information, make strong suggestions but not impose!" I was getting worked up.

"Honey! Will you start resenting wearing clothes because social norms put such authoritarian diktats on us? You are not trying to go nudist are you?"

"It's the principle of it, Neera!"

"Well sweetie" she calmed me down. "At such times of crisis, we need to look at the greater good of society. We do that here too, don't we?" Her eyes had that look in them, the two crescent brows slightly raised as if she was educating Mika. I don't mind it. I love her for exactly that.

"Not should, but ought to," I correct her. "Here, we do it by our choice. To each his own. It should be left to me to choose to protect myself and for the old man to protect himself. I should not impose my protection onto him unless he asks me." We continue with our different worldviews.

"Well, you can break all those stipulations later in the evening honey, no mask, no clothes, no nothing." She cheekily giggles as she pulls herself out of our embrace.

I can feel her anticipation for our evening date at the beach — our occasional trysts of risqué. None of her partners from the commune — Rudi, Idrissa, Jasper, or Vahana (well, Vahana is too old for such adventures) — give in to her naughty little fantasy of outdoor sex.

"I am not sure though how many people will be at the Santa Barbara beach during a weekday evening with this Corona scare," she says doubtfully.

Californians have adhered to social distancing much more religiously than the rest of the country.

Neera pauses at the door on her way out and turned around, a halo around her head so radiant from the light behind.

"Ooo! Then, how about East Beach Santa Barbara? That is gotta be more crowded!" Her eyes light up in anticipation.

IV

AND WHO SAID? —THE UNSAID
– Stella Hughes

East Beach is usually the less crowded part of Santa Barbara County Beach, especially if you move away from the hotels and towards the Refuge. It does not die down like the rest of the beach as the sun sets. There's always an occasional doting couple from the hotel or the inn who drift further east for privacy. But today, there are a few more people than that. At least more than in the last year of desolation. No matter what, the ambience at the beach is creating illusions about the time of evening, and not just because of the bustle. Darkness has set in but its influence has failed to prevail over the beachgoers.

Is it those lights far away across the water, crouching above the dark ocean surface — the dull grimy lights from the oilrigs ruining the pristine mystery of the Pacific? That can't be it. They seem too far away to masquerade as the streetlights for the beach. The distant lights just add to the hubbub of the people ambling along and the sound of the waves washing the sands, as the breeze wafts fragrances from their conversations. Some words from the conversations are more persistent than others — allusions to the rising cases of vaccine injuries, the masks, and the silver bullet — the antidote to the vaccine. Hope emanates from the conversations, some muffled from masks donned despite the freshness of the ocean breeze, others not. There are occasional streaks of resentment from those who had always mistrusted the vaccines and now the antidote — typecast into a social malevolent class, a pinhole-sized leak in inflated optimism. A leak nevertheless. This recently added hygiene practice has snowballed into a political stance where no tolerance is left for opinions on that insignificant practice. On the political front, some mentions of the bold measures by President Broderick drift over in the waft of ebullience.

But the toxicity from the acrimonious reign of the previous president has still not died down. The contrast of President Broderick's policies provides the fodder for the celebration. Especially here, amongst whom the animus towards the previous leader also announced their frustration of ending up on the leeward side of the democratic process. Their voice had finally surfaced this time in their choice in Broderick. It is indeed palpable even here, this late. Humans cannot stay restrained too long, lockdown after lockdown, resurgence after resurgence, election after election. The recent election was the real liberation the Californians are celebrating — the easing of restrictions from a vaccine-liberated populace is the dessert in the feast already in progress. Who had not loathed the narcissistic, whimsical ex-president who had started the dictatorial mass vaccination experiment in the first place? Even some who had erred on the side of casting their vote in his name have switched sides. But the Californians did it with a cathartic abhorrence, preferring to flip their opinions on any issue rather than be caught agreeing with his rare rational assessments. Public opinion is like a pendulum, swinging end to end.

Not me. I didn't vote for the dynamic Mr 'I can say the right words'. Not that I was a fan of the petty narcissist before him. But my traumatic history with President Broderick puts me between a rock and a hard place. But then commoners like me are expendable. Ignored victims of accidental trespassers — some repentant child molesters, as long as they repent, not repeat, dare not admit, and fit into the image of a chosen leader of the society at large. I am mere collateral damage of the momentum of their grand designs of 'greater-good' hurtling them to imminent fame.

As Neeraja loves to say, "In the end, they are all the same, Stella — one narcissist replaced by another. Why else do you think they pursue this fame? Why do you think they get anointed to such leadership roles? This whole business of 'the chosen one' is not my cup of tea."

With such ideology and iconoclastic views, she fits so well into the Nazarene Commune! But alas, she chose not to. Her choice is a loss for the commune, but a gain for the world at large and I daresay my gain?

Neeraja is very right about leaders though. Why do they choose to be leaders? Why do they choose to be chosen? If not convinced about their apparent 'meant to be', how would they convince the dumb masses of it? She is right, they are all narcissists in the end. If Broderick wasn't a narcissist convinced about his divine right over me, if he wasn't a narcissist convinced that he was above the rules of morality when he did those despicable things to my tender mind and put my innocent body to his lustful scrutiny, wouldn't he just be a petty criminal unconvinced about the morality of the world? And yet, since then, he has assumed a moral high ground on domestic crime — *'Patio and Inner-room crime'* as he has branded it — and taken an activist role in the prosecution of such and more horrendous domestic crimes. The very crime he was guilty of against me! *'Morality has no substitution nor a circumvention'* — his message throughout the eighteen years of his political career since. The very slogan that won him the election as he tight-rope-walked between the conservative religious and his liberal base.

"They just come with the same message, each one with a different twist." Rather ironic that Neeraja had said so just over a year ago, given who was sworn in as Broderick's Vice President!

The fragments of voices cushioned between the swoosh of the waves and the cool evening breeze also trend about the President's grand experiment — his sidekick, Vice President Neela. A twist of bitter lime in the summer breeze cocktails.

It suited Neeraja quite well. The people on the beach I mean. Since she returned from India, she has become a bit paranoid. Safety for women in dark desolate places is an issue in this country too. But I'd worry about it only in the inner cities — South Central in Los Angeles, Long Beach, Oakland, South Chicago, or San Francisco. Not here at the county beach. It still may not be as safe as in Europe or Japan or even the monarchic Middle East (except when you catch the fancy of someone with a bit of money and the clergy on their side) but I would come to this beach at any time of the night. Where I don't trust for the safety of a girl in this country is the safest of places — one's own house, in the safest of situations like a Quinzeñera party at home with amongst the most trusted people, Mom's most trusted colleagues and respectable senators jostling for more influence in the party. That bothers me more than beaches. But that just might be me.

Neeraja's paranoia is definitely coming from her stay in India. I am quite sure it is not against William. That couldn't be. They have a history. A good history I mean. Not like mine with Mr. Senator and now Mr. President. Shame on me! For tainting Neeraja and William's great history with horrendous slices of my teen memories. Their history is pristine despite the few whims and some pigheaded backlashes. Even if it cost them a decade and a half apart. Give or take.

True love is indeed rare and I can attest to its magical sparkly glow — that wee bit of Aurora Borealis that got captured by the sparks between them. The stubborn knot that connects them is indelible even while being invisible as if ageless, timeless, and ordained beyond the confines of spaces and expediency of time.

I do wonder what this rendezvous is about. I mean Neeraja rushing to Santa Barbara just days after her long flight from Delhi to San Francisco.

I mean she must be exhausted!

I have never been to India, but I do know that it is on the other side of the world. Almost night and day.

I've felt sorry for some of my colleagues in India during the many calls at the most ungodly hours there, just because it is at a decent hour here. Making them work at odd hours to serve us, their prosperity-bearers in the Land of the Free. Neeraja claims there is a lot more freedom in India. Was. Until this pandemic broke. Freedom at what cost though? And now the loss of it at what?

Neeraja said the police were patrolling everywhere in the country in the name of lockdown after lockdown. She's been there the last couple of years — an exile away from her ambivalent husband.

Exile for him or herself? It did help him make up his mind soon after about his identity. Or rather her identity. His, her, Their, whatever.

I am in sync with the current generation on this one. Why this emphasis on the pronoun for an identity or even the gender? My convictions come on a more metaphysical level. Far deeper than even notions professed by Pappa Y. His are on a spiritual level — gender as an ID or permit for procreation and extending into a mere natural proclivity. Pappa Y is right on that level. He's seldom wrong on anything on that level anyway.

"Why hinge around an identity that a human needs for a mere nature's chore?!" Pappa Y has often proclaimed in his intoned sermons.

"Do you base your judgment of a person on the shape of his nose, just because he wheezes a bit while breathing? Or on what he prefers to eat? Or drink? Or how he prefers to take a dump?" Pappa Y loves to veer towards the crass for shock value, but also because he attaches no importance to the 'hierarchy of words defining superfluous charades of modesty'. His own words again. He is just great. He says the right words too. But with more candor and a lot more earnestness. At a much deeper level.

I didn't start out as his greatest fan. I did not join the Nazarene commune as a big fan of him or his teachings. I hardly knew or understood his teachings. Even if I pretended back then to William that I did. Why I joined the commune is an open secret. Open to everyone except Neeraja, and I suspect not a secret to William either. But the last twelve years in the Commune have made me more receptive and a lot more devoted to Pappa Y's philosophy and spirituality. Not just about gender identity, but about everything of meaning in life on this planet.

My views about gender identity go further, deeper, and more sublime. Right to the level of consciousness. For consciousness has no props of identity. Not in gender or anything physical. It is so much more nascent. If only more people could feel their consciousness as their identity. If only this generation knew. If only most humans of this generation were even aware of this. But luckily, they are not so rigid about gender identity even if they have no clue why. And that is a start in the right direction.

Neeraja doesn't belong to what I would call this generation. She missed it only by a couple of years. Perhaps that is why she needed an escape. It was tough on her. More so since the pandemic broke out or perhaps since her husband moved into the limelight as the VP candidate, but definitely after her husband finally came out of the closet. Or maybe not. She did after all move away with her daughter to insulate him from his two biggest weaknesses — herself and Mika. It was definitely the pandemic. The lockdowns take the cake on any list of challenges. She was complaining about how stringent the lockdown was in India.

"So many food trolleys, laundry kiosks, street-side businesses forced to shut down. While the white-collared comfortably earn their big bucks, bunkered down from the diabolical virus; the teachers, the food-stand owners, and the many self-employed home-help took a plunge towards poverty to protect the prosperous homeowners from infection."

"Infected with what?" William cracked up the last time I brought it up to him just a few weeks ago at the commune. "Do you know how many epidemics that tropical country has every monsoon? I mean it's not that their suite of pathogens is less deadly. They are ten-fold deadlier than Covid — Malaria, Dengue fever, Meningitis, Salmonella, and Chikungunya! Yeah! They even have this disease that sounds more like a chicken curry!" He said in an undertone.

I may be a big Willie fan, but it's not for his sense of humor. Only the Big-willie part. His jokes are always awkward, a bit contrived — even about the most intimate moments in bed. Not really funny, if you know what I mean. But he is funny in bed, even if not with his words.

Long ago, more than a decade and a half ago, Neeraja used to coo about William. "Willie is such a riot! Wait till you meet him." Little did she know how the future would unfold. But not as far as his humor goes. Not for me.

I think she was just head-over-heels in love with him. In some ways she still is. So is William, in his own headstrong, fortuitous way. I always perceived that warm glow in him, every time we converged on that topic. How can we not? Neeraja is the elephant in the room whenever William and I hook up. Not that I feel guilty about it. The petite slim beauty with dark big eyes — a benign enigma, tantalizing in the glow of her black pupils amidst the shining whites, bearing all the affection of optimism for the better of the world around her and even beyond, is always a treat around, even as a 20-ton elephant lurking in a room steamed up from hours of our lovemaking.

"And despite those deadly pathogens and the epidemics they face so regularly — they are still a billion! A billion people scared of a flu-like virus!" He charged indignantly. His habit of simplifying everything into a few sweeping judgments.

Perhaps it is just a man thing, unable to recognize the different shades and different colors that make up the whole issue; understanding the fear of death or suffering that riddles humans, no matter how many times they have fallen sick before. The instinctive fear of mortality. Understanding the human behavior and that too in this connected world of social media, where keeping up with Joneses is no longer about rubbing shoulders with the successful Mr Jones of the block, but the thousands and millions of status updates and check-ins that we read and envy every day as a morning coffee routine. If the rich white countries locked down their people no longer exposed to a broad suite of bacteria, the other countries follow suit, to keep up with the Joneses.

"I am glad she is coming back. She needs to deal with the reality of N..." and he hurriedly corrected himself, "Vice President Neela." He said it saltily, still not sure how to refer to Neeraja's husband.

They are still technically married. Neela the VP with the lamp, as she is called adoringly, for her endeavor to finally solve the aftermath we are facing from the panic mass vaccination that is unleashing all the complications, one at a time. It doesn't end! But then Neela's promised antidote is the hope that has energized everyone.

Neela was after all trained in Autoimmunology at John Hopkins, back when she was Neel and was still coveted for his eligible bachelor status in the American Indian arranged marriage world.

Meanwhile, William is still not over Neeraja dumping him for a traditional arranged husband many years ago.

"Willie picked Pappa Y over me." She had burst out a few days after she agreed to the arranged marriage proposal from Neel's folks to her parents, fifteen years ago. She was interning for me back then. For her it was simple — if her Willie loved her, he would have proposed to her rather than cajoling her to join the Nazarene commune. And in that, she was just not fair to him. I am not siding with him on this. I am just saying that it is never that simple. It's not as simple as that. William knows it. So do I. Everyone except Neeraja knows. It was never that simple, but in her mind — it was. Open and shut.

It happened during a wild 40 hours after his graduation party. He has shared it with me so many times. It still lurks in his head — those 40 hours. For him, it is the passionate buildup before the big plunge.

"If only!" He groans every time, without actually saying those words.

Apparently, she had alluded to where their 'plans' were heading. It was a *fait-accompli* for her — the whole marriage thing. They were meant to be. It was for him too, I suspect, on some paradoxical level. As an afterthought to his traumatic reflections of the evening, I can surmise that. It is just that he was dumb enough not to see the imminence of it.

Not dumb as a person. I wouldn't have fallen for him if he was dumb. I mean dumb, just as any man is about these things. And he tried to lure her away from their anticipated knot to the life at the commune by bringing up his job offer from Pappa Y. You see what I mean by dumb as any man?!

And yet here they are! William and Neeraja! In a clandestine rendezvous on the East Beach Santa Barbara, at 9 pm on a weekday, amidst the grand celebration of liberty two times over! No fireworks or any of that sort, but the spirit is insurmountable — even in California and despite the impending drought.

And all that through my machinations — conscious and unconscious. And it did not even weird me out. It probably should I guess, but it didn't. Strangely. I wasn't even feeling nervous about it, given their history and my present with William.

But what happens at the Commune stays at the commune.

Ewwww! It's not like the Vegas thing. No way! For one thing, it is nowhere as superfluous as Vegas. And in many ways, in fact, all ways, Nazarene is the exact opposite of what Vegas stands for. Although, the liaisons at the commune are not any stickier than the weddings at a Vegas Chapel. In that, there is some similarity but for the exact opposite reasons. Here, the news stays in the commune simply because it is not important enough to be announced to the prudish puritanical world outside. Nothing at Nazarene is. Everything is merely a routine part of life, I mean all the bodily chores. Would one gossip about the showers we take? Or the hiccups we have once in a while? Or the flatulence (taking a page out of Pappa Y's book)? But I say that in more earnestness than him. There are enough older men at the commune. Anyone who has had even one of the original founding members of the commune as a partner — and trust me, most of us have, given the lifestyle here — knows why I dared to bring up flatulence. But none of that is worth gossiping about. We just get on with it. Life has far more to it than such uneventful couplings.

For me, it is still not going far enough. Yeah, sure! Pappa Y's emphasis on more important things in life —spirituality, life at its moment, and whatever he has picked up from Advaita, his foster spiritual home, has its moments. But then most people, if they went far enough beyond it would not be able to handle life in its transience. I have been living with it. I mean everyone is living with it, they just don't realize it. I do and have no qualms about it. It is my purpose.

But this is not about me. It is about rekindling the celestial flame between the two of them — William and Neeraja. I am just happy to play my part in making it happen. In some strangely unconscious, conniving happenstance, I plunged into the commune with an honest crush on him back then, to perhaps be that buffer during their long impasse. But the time had come.

East Beach though was not my suggestion. It was proposed by one of them that I just conveyed to the other.

As the waves break the silence of darkness into a mischievous purl, the first moment of their tete-a-tete is palpable. Beyond palpable. It is charged. Charged with the impetus of destiny gathered over from not just this instance, but many such; from many lives over in many realities. Not anyone else's lives. Their own lives, many lives, all converging at this momentous rendezvous. Even the hubbub cannot jolt away from the charge.

"Gosh! It's not as quiet as I thought it would be," Neeraja confesses, in a hurry to speak even before she could unwind their hug. True, such physical displays of greeting have become taboo in the last year. But not for them, not between them, where time comes to a standstill.

"Says the woman returning from a country of a billion and half." William has his urges of hyperbole. She merely rolls her eyes, not in exasperation, as they reluctantly unwind their extended hug.

It is not that they are at the Flat Iron on Broadway. It is, as Neeraja mentioned, the fragments of conversations and muffled words drifting across the sandy expanse, occasionally broken by the splash of the waves gently whipping the sand grains. The presence of people is merely notional.

"And I thought you preferred the presence of people, the risk of being seen," his impudent snide smile taunting her.

"Willie," she shushes him with a coy slap on his wrist, while quickly checking over her shoulder.

They pick up where they had left off more than fifteen years ago.

And I rest my case!

"How've you been, Neera?!" He transitions not that smoothly, as he rubs her right arm with his wrist. "Gosh! I thought I wouldn't see you in a million years when I heard you left for India. Thought you would not return — you always fit in so well there. So at home in your home." He laughs in a hurry, not sure if it was needed here, but nevertheless trying to camouflage whatever else he was trying to desperately mask.

But before Neeraja can complete her negation,

"Not anymore Willie. I feel like a fish out of water there now",

William continues, talking right through her confession,

"But then Broderick chose Neel as his running mate, so I guess you needed to be back. You have been in the news for the last few months, y'know. Almost a celebrity" he is gushing.

"Neela…" She immediately corrects him and continues in a hushed tone, as if that was necessary, "And that's why I chose this beach, Willie. Thought there wouldn't be so many people here. No one to recognize me. I guess I was wrong, about people, I mean," Neeraja explains.

"You? fish out of what now?" William hurries to break the awkward silence, more to kick sand over any hints of his vulnerability.

"Fish out of water in Udaipur…?" William continues after a hurried dismissal with his frown, "Seriously, Neera? Why? How can you be uncomfortable there? It's your home! Your eyes used to light up at the very thought of Rajasthan. At the faintest notes of that mournful instrument, whatchamacallit it — Saarangi!" He snaps his fingers. "Your eyes would shine like two beautiful flames even in the darkest nights to those raspy folk melodies." And then he breaks into a folk tune, carving it out of his memory.

"*Paddaro Maare desh re…*" From Neeraja's silent wince in the darkness, I gather that his enunciation was terrible. American accents put a death knell on the best and worst bits of any vernacular articulation.

"You remember it, Willie?" Her eyes flash like two cozy beacons from the dark dampness of the ocean breeze, and the lights from the rig cower in retreat to the glow of her eyes. "It's from my cousin's wedding, eighteen years ago!"

"No, this was not at your Jiji's[1] wedding," William corrects her, every moment from that long ago still vivid in his memory. Not the William I am familiar with — that William has the memory of a goldfish.

"Remember the concert your..." he gropes for the right phrase, or perhaps pauses to recollect, "...your *Bua*[2] took us to?"

"My Bua?!" Neeraja is shell-shocked, perhaps not so much that he remembered where exactly the tune was played almost two decades ago, while they were still in Graduate School, but that he remembers her Aunt by how she calls her.

Sometimes it doesn't take much for tears to well up in a woman's eyes — in a woman as earnest, intense, and passionate as Neeraja. But this is not one of those instances.

Today, there is a larger context. 1. The last few months of despair as people near her, and some dear to her, succumbed to the ravages of the pandemic in India and in the most pitiable circumstances too, where city authorities kept the departed cadaver as a pestilence, depriving it of a funeral dignity. 2. Two years of exile from a man, who in his lifelong struggle with an identity the society had slapped onto him for a merely twisted coupling of two doubly twisted DNA, had failed them both in marriage. 3. The dilemma of keeping a brave face in her native society that judged

---

1 Older female cousin or sister

2 Aunt from father's side

a woman on her nuptial fortunes while enabling her man to confront his femininity boldly.

And news such as this: of the most powerful man on earth choosing an Indian American and one of an alternate gender, as his running mate had flooded every news channel in India. The cat was out of the bag after that. There was little she could do to conceal anything from her family. 4. The sheer weight of the wisdom of her soul as a wife, a conscientious empathetic companion, a responsible mother, and an abstracted inamorata in denial. 5. On top of all that she was battling to quell the gossip and speculations arising from her absence at the presidential inaugural gala a few months ago.

I have to confess, my country is a nation so hellbent on extricating itself from its colonial ancestry, some social celebrations at the helm aped a bit too much out of the chapters from *Pride and Prejudice* or any other Edwardian ball.

There were many layers of burden piled onto her resilient self, least of which was the harsh reality that her husband was most likely picked for the leadership role of the free world, more as a qualifier for as many checkboxes rather than actual merit that Neela's resumé could proudly announce — agreeably, checkboxes broadcasting brave statements against prejudice and discrimination in a country rife with conservative prejudices, but nevertheless mere political posture. All of this put heavy onus on this compassionate glowing soul.

Tears trickle down her dusky cheeks as rivulets while she smiles adoringly at her Willie. In the darkness that prevails at the beach though, Willie is clueless.

"What do you mean Bua?! Why wouldn't I remember Meenakshi Bua?!" William drives in, carefully chewing Neeraja's Dad's sister's name, a rather tongue-twister for any outsider, flourishing his impeccable memory from his first and only visit to India — a trip that sealed their love affair decades ago.

"I was very ..." but Neeraja does not let him finish his flourish. When she seals her lips onto his, it is indeed to silence him. Sometimes a man, even the most adorable one, just does not know when to shut up!

It is often said that the blatant and often brutish aggression in masculinity that a woman is so attracted to comes from the steroid portion in the testosterone. One must not forget that progesterone percolating through the feminine nature does have a steroid character to it as well.

Neeraja takes a step forward, snakes her right hand over his upper chest around his neck bringing his face down by her palm around his nape, and tiptoeing seizes his lower lip with her mouth, tears still streaming down her cheeks.

When it rains, it pours.

I've known Neeraja over the years and rather well as her boss, when she was interning. And I never saw her as a take-charge kinda woman. I used to observe her with men-in-power or otherwise, and she has always tended to cede the illusion of control over to the man even if patronizingly so. Not a morsel of eagerness to grab the wheel and take over. She had great potential to be a future leader who leads by example. A compassionate, empathetic person and an amazing mentee, she absolutely is! But not the one who grabbed the bull by the horns.

If this goldfish of a man had managed to remember *my* aunt from fifteen years ago and some exotic tunes from back then, I would drop out of the Nazarene, and pin him down into an exclusive myself.

I totally get the fire in her. An admission of love one gets back from her lover is the biggest aphrodisiac.

The rather obvious temperatures ignite rapidly on the beach. And I feel proud of myself for instrumenting this tryst. At this quick turn of events though, I am a bit lost about my original intent. This was not supposed to be a clandestine reunion of former lovers, but something more important, even if undisclosed, is what Neeraja or William had individually indicated to me. Perhaps it was subliminal, their intent, and my avowal.

"Do you think he'd be willing to meet me in the next couple of weeks? I need to sort out some things with him," she had said over the phone after she landed back in DC. "Things I have kept off too long."

"Since you broke up with him??! 15 years is a long silence Neeraja," I said, trying my best to be the trusted protégé I've always seen myself as. She treats me as her friend though.

"Good gosh no! We met a few times after that, in my first year of marriage. I did want him to have closure. And me as well. Then a couple more times, during a trip to San Francisco." She was drifting off into reminiscences, I could feel it on the phone.

"But not after that." She was deliberately putting finality into that phrase. But then she again broke her brief silence.

"Do you think he would meet me?" She seemed very apprehensive and I was surprised why? Nothing I got from William ever suggested he wouldn't. What state did she leave him in that she feared incurring his wrath? Did she not know her Willie as well as I knew her William? He is a puppy, despite his heaving chest, despite those confident braggy drawls, and his free-spirited hot manliness. He is an adorable puppy that I have no qualms in trading off for the greater good that spans a wider truth and a heavier reality. Or should I say realities?

"Of course, he will" I had said but decided to hedge it, not give away the current state of affairs between her ex-lover and me. "I mean, I don't see why not. As I told you, he is no stranger to me. I mean, no one at the commune can be. And anytime you have come up in our conversations, I've observed nothing that would suggest otherwise."

And then on a whim, —well not really a whim but more based on a purposeful hunch that pervaded my intuition of just the then and now — I volunteered.

"Just tell me when you will be in town and I will make sure he meets you, Neeraja. It seems rather important to you and I think you have a lot on your plate. Happy to get this done for you."

"What do you mean 'a lot on your plate?" She seemed a bit defensive and honestly, quite edgy.

"I mean now that you are back for good and having to move to DC and all that," I explained, not quite convincing myself. But she agreed.

She had suggested a less public place and I think William had suggested the East beach. "It is not a long drive from the commune and she likes that kind of a place." He had an impish smile when he said it.

And that was it. It was supposed to be an innocuous tete-a-tete to sort out some stuff that she had been keeping off.

But here they are in the throes of passionate moans and carnal spasms, making me feel like a trans-medium voyeur of some sort just for narrating it, even if I am not actually eavesdropping.

And like that, hours pass by, as darkness seals its grip over the beach, once the conversations around the beach die down. Neeraja and William have found a quiet piece of turf and a bench, and languish there semi-dressed — her head on his shoulder as he diligently tangles his fingers through the long glossy strands of her dark hair.

"Is this why you stopped?" He has a certain smugness about him. She turns over her side, as she rests her chin on his chest, taking an eyeful of him into her black iris, making it very meaningful and wise in the mischief they glisten with.

"Because we end up like this every time we meet." He has a triumphant air about him, but empathy makes its presence known.

He glances down at her radiant meaningful eyes. "But this time it was you who seduced me," he smiles at her accusingly.

"Yes, this is why I stopped." Her head nods and bobs up and down, as she speaks with her chin supporting her head on his chest. Her eyes still glisten in a bit of amusement, a bit of mischief, and a whole lot of bliss, "because you can't keep your hands off me but end up blaming me."

"Blaming you for what?"

"I can't keep my hands off either," she makes her sardonic confession, once again both finishing at the same time.

"For my marital infidelity," and as she mouths that, even as he pulls her by shoulders into a long drawn kiss, her eyes cloud at the weight of what she just said. But she doesn't pull herself away and continues indulging in the languishing sweetness of his lips.

"Marital infidelity," he cackles. "After the turn of events in the last two years, I would certainly not blame you for that particular sin." He eyes her to see her reaction to his provocative statement, adding fondly, "I never blamed you for that ever, Neera! Even when your sudden silence after the last time shattered me, I never blamed you. It just made me rationalize our fling after Neel came out."

"Neela." She corrects him again.

"We need to stop this, Willie. We can't go on like this every time we meet." She stirs into an unknown decision but does nothing to break their languid intimacy.

She lets Willie's annoyed silence linger, but then he stirs and tries to extricate himself from the bench. He takes the voice of her finality as her gavel of final rejection of him.

She rises slightly and pivots herself, straddles him while her hands pin him down by his shoulders. Despite his size, he feels Neeraja's sheer strength of will as she presses his shoulders down, her golden necklace with an emerald pendant and two miniature gold saucers — the symbol of her Hindu marriage, swinging tantalizingly above his chin.

"We need to put a stop to these illicit affairs, Willie. I can't go on with these brief run-ins twelve years apart and then run away in my guilt. I want to put a stop to this guilt. Even these momentary spates." This is not why she had arranged this meeting with

William. This is definitely not what she wants to sort out. This is definitely extemporaneous.

He turns his face away, perhaps not to look weak. Neither in his emotions nor his strength, having been pinned down and unable to walk away. She softly pecks his check close enough to his mouth, which is turned away in a sulk. It was more of a tender caress with her lips — to put his fear of another rejection to rest.

"I like these brief spates so much better than the rest of my life, Willie. The rest of my life has become such a sham. But this is not why I like these spates, Willie. I always liked them. Even back then, those two days twelve years ago."

"I love Neela and I always vowed to support her even before she came out. But I don't want to go living this sham. Not for Mika. She deserves better. And not for my second baby, I don't want her to be born in living an illusion, Willie."

William turns his face and regards her head to chest, momentarily distracted by the wide-open cove pushed near his face.

"You are pregnant?!"

"I most certainly think so." She smiles at him.

"You haven't taken the test yet?" He is searching and thinking.

She shakes her head amused.

He thinks for a bit and sighs in disbelief, almost in disappointment.

"How?!" And as he makes another vain attempt to wrestle free from under her,

"Who?"

She smiles amused, as she puts the full weight of her torso onto her hands to hold him back as his attempt to rise becomes more fervent, "I feel quite certain I just conceived. Now!" She gives a dramatic pause and regards his hopeless dismissal, desperate to believe her but urging himself to somehow dismiss it in his huff.

"I am not wrong on this one" There is again that husky lilt of certainty in her voice.

William sighs in disbelief but stops resisting.

"That's your excuse?" His voice is muffled under the dense blanket of her hair, as she bends and rests her head on his shoulder again, not letting go of her gaze.

"I can't, Willie. I can't. This pretense that I am happily married and Mika, and now the baby."

William cackles, shaking his head. And then sobers up.

"I am sorry I shouldn't be laughing. But think of your Mika. She has two mothers and I am sure she will grow up through it and be proud of both her mothers. And this new baby," he regarded her and flashed a mocking smile, "her half-sister that isn't Neela's kid. How are you going to explain that? And how are you going to remain married? Just because she is a Vice

President now? Oh Gosh! Your life is such a mess, Neera!"

But he stops short and reaches his palm out to her cheek and caresses it. "Don't complicate your life any further, Neera. Stop dreaming about a new baby. Bring Mika up properly. It must be complicated for her already. She is what? Ten?"

"Eleven," Neeraja replies and it comes back to her. Through the throes of passion, her irresistible attraction to Willie, and her desire to have him then and there, she realizes why she wanted to sort things out.

But she lets Willie's odor, as she draws her breath close to his ear and cheek, seep into her being. The silence lingers. William is reflecting on the gravity of her juxtaposition, or at least what he thinks is her juxtaposition in a marriage with now a woman holding the second-highest office of the land. And what it means for his beloved Neera. She let the silence linger as she gathers her thoughts about why she had arranged the rendezvous.

"Had I? Or did Stella? Did Stella influence me into this?" Neeraja isn't sure but the very fact that she is unraveling that whole process of this rendezvous is cathartic.

I don't mind the blame on me. I have nothing to fear. It is not I who is carrying any guilt. She is. Even if a benevolent one. I had not influenced the rendezvous out of design or connivance. It was an unconscious insistence that panned many realities, across many could-haves and should-haves that my identity as Stella had instrumented by merely being so. By cozily fitting into the complex mosaic of their entangled lives in every possible reality and making sure that they coupled for some greater truth in posterity.

But Neeraja does circle back to what she wanted to sort out. And she wants more.

"I need to put an end to this sham, Willie. Not my marriage. That never took off anyway. Even though Neela and I care about each other so much. Always will. This sham that I belong with Neela just because you rejected me. This sham that Mika's dad is Neela, even when Neela knows she is not. This sham that we had a history and just a history. I want to stop it, Willie. It just being history."

She pulls herself up and straddles back, in command, as she reaches out with both her hands, palms caressing William's cheeks, her black soulful enlightened eyes burning deep into his blue eyes, the burning pain of love ignited in immortal desire that William drinks without a flinch.

"I want to put a stop to this whole humbug as to what we are to each other that we both always dismiss. We belong together, Willie. You, me, OUR Mika, and our second baby." She is definitely in control now.

"She is eleven?!" William regards her thoughtfully, a streak of pride sneaking into his eyes. Neeraja's long eyelashes momentarily fan down in affirmation.

"Mika is your daughter Willie. She always was, always will be. And for her, You and I were always meant to be. It's time we stop fighting it. We always will be us, always are, always were, no matter where, no matter when."

Even I couldn't have put it in better words myself than through her. The eternal truth and perhaps my raison-d'être. Not my only one, but an important one.

V

THE EPITAPH ACROSS THE WORLDS
– Stella Hughes

Is this what I was meant to be? — A sad interlude to the grand harmony of the coalescing passions of the entangled souls of Neeraja and William? A mere pawn in the grand finale of a love story?

In a grander scheme of things, in an uncountable melee of billions of 'meant to-be's, I guess everyone, every bit of consciousness that takes on a constant identity of a soul in this universe, scattering itself around spatially as well as temporally across the different versions of reality, is merely a small piece in the big jigsaw puzzle.

'We are all mere strands in the web of life,' Chief Seattle had said.

To President Pierce in a letter in one version.

To Governor Stevens in a speech in yet another.

And many versions of that did indeed occur — not in archives of history but in the grand reality of multiverses. And in some versions, the state of Washington never came to be for another hundred years. In all versions of reality though, Chief Seattle died in a hopeless sense of defeat— in one way or another for exceeding his limits as a strand and selling out the web that he so steadfastly felt himself a part of.

The love story of Neeraja and William too is persistent in its destiny no matter what version. No matter if great or grand or none of that, but for that web of love, I was a privileged strand.

Standing testimony to Neeraja and William's imminent destiny — no matter what, no matter where and no matter when; announces itself in an obscure grand tombstone on Planet Lydia in the Capella Star system of the constellation of Auriga,

'Here lies the Queen of Lydia, Mohini Kashyap Babbitt of the Blue Planet of the Solar System of The Orion Cygnus Arm. The great seductress & liberator of Life. The one who seduced a truce between the intimidatingly incipient indulgences of the intelligent Viruses and their symbiotic larger cognitive-being victims, in all planets she graced her soul with. The Angel who bridged the arrogance of all cognizant life in the Outer Milky Way neighborhoods with the simplicity of the ubiquitous protozoan intelligence. OH, THAT! AND HER SEDUCTIVE CHARM!'

It is said that she seduced the guile connivance out of the superior Viruses with her charm and tricked them into a truce with the dumber multi-cellular cognitive beings, sometimes known as Humans and other vain inhabitants across the Galaxy.

The tomb has gathered much dust on a sandy planet, on a star system in the neighboring arm of the galaxy, only a few thousand light-years away. Life may have dried to dust there, but life prevails in neighborhood planets, on earth, and across other galactic worlds and owes it to Queen Mohini Kashyap Babbitt; that she was born at all, despite multiple possibilities.

********************* END *********************

A NOTE ABOUT THE AUTHOR

Shashi Alur (1969-2022) was, by education and profession, a civil engineering and management specialist. After graduating from the National Institute of Technology, Warangal (Telengana, India) with a B.Tech degree in Civil Engineering, he worked for a few years in Muscat (Oman); He then moved to the US to pursue a management degree in International Management from Thunderbird (Pheonix, Arizona) and eventually worked there in the Corporate Consultancy Program (CCP) for 8 years. As a member of the CCP team, he visited various countries in Europe, Asia, and South America. He later moved to Basel, Switzerland to work with Strauman, a dental implant firm, as a Management Consultant. During the last few years of his life in Basel, he worked as a Visiting Lecturer for EHL, a Hospitality Management Institute at Lausanne, Switzerland. Besides writing articles on management issues in professional journals and making presentations at conferences, he followed his creative interests, writing poems and short articles. In addition to this novella, he has a novel (a manuscript) on Magda, a musical icon, awaiting publication.